Darwin, Singer

by Nadria Tucker

Sixteenth Avenue Books | Birmingham

Darwin, Singer

Copyright © 2012 by Nadria Tucker

ISBN-13: 978-0-9849013-1-9
ISBN-10: 0984901310

Cover design copyright © 2012 by Jamie Harper

Editor | Jason Horn

For my parents, who taught me to read
anything
and appreciate
everything.

Part I

One day, about thirteen years ago,
an employee followed an order.

1.

The stadium vibrates with the sound of a hundred thousand people in gray, packed shoulder to shoulder, screaming as loud as they can, louder than they should. But there's enough space to sit between Cicero (Wordsmith, a writer, obviously) and Newton (Stringer—the best musician in our class of initiates, a whiz at guitar, violin, theorbo, psaltery, zither). The lanky guitar player's become a regular fixture in life since he and Cicero struck up a friendship working on a project together. He's okay—his rebellious streak might be a good influence on Cicero, whose always perfectly pressed grays never cease to dispel my sneaking suspicion that she spends her spare time creating a giant list of all my character flaws (including a tendency to hoard brightly colored socks) and waiting for the perfect moment to use them against me in an epic roommate battle royale.

D.C. vs. L.A.: the biggest rivalry in the league. Today's the first time Newton's managed to drag us out to a game. He says his roommates are both sick, and he put on this ridiculous pouty face that for some reason Cicero finds herself unable to refuse. We sit on the D.C. side, since we live in Washington and are wards (soon to be full-time employees) of the state. The stadium's right in the center of D.C.'s Pleasure District, home to restaurants and bars that stay open late. With a capacity of a hundred thousand, and with D.C. up by seven at the half, the stadium—the whole district actually—thunders with noise.

"Late, as usual." Cicero's idea of a pleasant greeting.

The cold stings more than the criticism. A clear winter night like this usually makes for perfect football weather, but now, with the price hike on down coats, who can afford to dress for a freeze every day? Not a sixteen-year-old initiate saving up for integration expenses like rent, furniture, freedom parties . . .

"I got buried under a pile of laundry."

A lie. What started as an interweb search on meditation and other relaxation techniques—integration into civilian society after years of living a strict, state-controlled life tends to stress a person out—devolved into a session of random clicking, which led to a 50-year-old text on pre-WI art and a whole day of reading. The text scrolling across our dorm room's media screen gave a brief history on the types of art banned by the Wagner Initiative. A landmark case in Florida: Musicians were charged with violating obscenity laws for playing a concert and performing songs about sex. The state, surprisingly, found the group not guilty, but the trial led to a series of similar trials all over the country in the following decades. With each case, the movement that became the WI gained momentum, the typical verdict changed from "not guilty" to "guilty," and eventually obscenity in all forms disappeared.

Cicero and Newton don't need to know about the marathon reading session on Non-Approved Art. Especially since we, as members of the WI, are supposed to hate, despise, loathe and report any instances of NAA we come across. Not that any of us have ever seen (or heard) any banned art. NAA probably doesn't even exist anymore. Who'd be stupid enough to try it? And risk prison? No way.

"What's the plot?"

"Some of the Los Angeles players got bounced out of a bar last night. If I'd been there . . ." Newton pretends to put a football player in a headlock—not a convincing sight with his skinny arms. "They blamed it on D.C. using their state connections to pull strings with the bar owner, but everyone knows that this year L.A. are rowdy, and lazy. The entire team got kicked out of their hotel in Michigan last week because they didn't clean the bathrooms before checkout." You'd think it was Newton's own bathroom left dirty by the disgust in his voice. "Michigan won that game and D.C.'s favored to win this one. Our team built a park for orphans last week."

And he's right. D.C. easily comes away with the win. Newton's always super-excited about the SFL, but results always seem so . . . predictable. Whichever team behaves better that week wins the game. Last year, Denver's team donated its entire profit margin to the state and came away with the national championship. No one claims football to be fair, but millions of people spend time and hard-earned demerits on it every weekend. I can think of better ways to spend my valuable time (rehearsing, for one). But it is sort of gratifying to see the good guys come out on top.

The short way from the stadium back to the dorm cuts straight through the center of the Pleasure District. Celebrations in restaurants and bars overflow into the streets. Cheering, laughing, hugging, civs in their D.C. colors, their red, white, and blue striped socks pulled way up over their pants, all the way to their knees.

"Dress code violations everywhere. Look at that."

Cicero points out a teenage girl who, despite rules (and the cold) wears red, white, and blue socks with a short gray skirt that ends well above the approved length, showing much more of her thigh than it should.

"Never seen that before." Newton doesn't seem too upset about it.

"Pick your jaw up off the ground."

Fascinating. This civ's willing to risk confinement to wear what she wants. Or . . . there's another possibility—rumor is the state sometimes plants improperly dressed agents undercover in the field to give them better access to civs who break the code and who refuse to report violations. The girl in the short skirt could be a plant. No matter. Cicero, always on the case, calls the automated dress-code violation line and reports the girl's presence.

There used to be a time without a state-enforced dress code. When I was six, already three years into my training, we took a rare field trip to watch a WI opera about treating others with respect. Sounds usually stick out—the crinkle of paper when I unfolded my first love note from a boy, the thwack of the paddle as the instructor punished the boy for disrupting choir practice—but my memory of the opera trip is mute. No melodies or roars of applause come to mind. Only colors— actors draped in layers of red velvet and pink silk, their lips painted bright red, the scenery behind them shining with glittery, green trees. Six-year-old me, waiting to meet the performers after the show, smoothing the wrinkles out of my state-issued soycloth dress. Purple. The memory might not even be real.

The crowd in the streets thins as we walk through the Pleasure District, into District A, D.C.'s nicest neighborhood. The homes of wealthy D.C. residents—high-ranking state officials, capitalists, and celebrity members of the WI—sit way back from the streets, three- or four-story townhouses made entirely of concrete (one of a few WI-approved exterior building materials, the others being glass and steel). In front of every house is a tall fence, topped with razor wire. You never can be too safe—you can't trust anyone, not even your rich neighbors.

The wind picks up, and a flurry of snow blows past. We hurry into the subsidized housing district, District B, block after block of interconnected rectangles and cubes—tall apartment buildings that hold most of D.C.'s population. WI employees usually move into one of these skyrises after their integration and spend the rest of their lives moving from apartment to slightly bigger apartment.

"Looks clean." Not really a selling point to anyone but Cicero.

"Of course it's clean," says Newton. "It's maintained by the state."

"It looks boring. Hundreds of blocks of identical apartments." Identical people sleeping inside, tucked into their identical sleeping pods, alongside their matching families.

"You're joking, right? No guards at the doors like there are back at the WI dorms. We'll be able to do whatever we want!" Newton practically jumps up and down at the thought.

"I don't know what sort of *whatever* you're thinking about doing, but I wouldn't, if I were you. The doors may not have guards, but there are enough cameras around that they'd catch you before you got up to anything. Look." Cicero points out three surveillance cameras on lampposts and corners trained in the group's general direction. And that's just on a single block.

"Whatever happened to privacy?" It'd be nice to use the bathroom without thinking someone might be watching, for once.

"Privacy leads to crimes. D.C.'s felony rate dropped by half when the state doubled its camera usage."

"Living in District B won't be much better than the dorms."

"So, what? Stay in the dorms? I don't think anyone's done it before, but I'm sure the WI would make an exception. And I do find the routine comforting."

It's not hard to picture the pale writer with her always miraculously styled red hair folding laundry in our dorm room for the rest of her life. An 80-year-old with a curfew.

"Maybe we could live somewhere else." The words come out before I can stop them.

"Yeah that's it. We'll pick a house in District A, break in, and crash in their spare bedroom." Newton puts his wrists in imaginary handcuffs.

"What about the Atlas District?"

A sharp left turn. Instead of heading for the dorms, now it's toward a place none of us have ever been, even though we all know the way.

"You can't be serious." Cicero jogs a few steps to catch up. "We're not . . ."

"I'm absolutely serious."

Newton follows. "I'm in!"

Cicero turns to Newton. "Have you been to the Atlas District?"

"Well . . . I've been near it. Not exactly *to* it."

"Well, let me educate you. They say it's filled with organized crime. If you go by yourself, you never come back."

Nothing's ever as bad as "they" say it is. Cafeteria food? Decent. That cheesy love history about Cleopatra and Marc Anthony? The best thing the WI's filmed in years. My taste is without a doubt better than "theirs." "It can't be that bad. At least there's someplace left in the city that still has character."

"You've lost your mind. Hear that, WI? Star vocalist Darwin Singer has officially gone bananas."

"That's right, WI. Cicero Wordsmith finally has what she's always wanted—a good reason to turn me in. Why can't you trust that I'm not using my lack of ironing skills to bring down the whole government?"

"Why can't you trust that I'm not an informant sent to spy on you and report your refusal to alphabetize the vitamins and cotton swabs?"

We reach a dead end. Behind us, the bland skyrises of District B climb into the night. In front of us, a street stretches out of sight in either direction, lined with squat buildings butting up against each other, some painted in peeling shades of yellow, red, and green, others left unadorned, the age of the building materials showing at the crumbling corners of bricks and stones.

People fill the street, wandering in and out of bars, restaurants, coffee shops, standing around (loitering!!) in front of storefronts, talking. In the middle of it all is a building so completely unlike anything else in the city. If you hadn't seen pictures of it in a history book before, you might think it had fallen from space—a small building plastered with posters advertising popular history films, topped with layers of decorative curves, all lit up, crowned with a giant neon sign that reads ATLAS in blue letters. An old-fashioned theater, the kind that used to show NAA films about fictional wars and made-up alien invasions— maybe the last theater like it left on Earth. A life-sized statue of a portly, bearded man stands guard outside the theatre, a smile playing across his wide mouth, making his cheeks look extra chubby—B.C. Atlas himself, according to the plaque at the statue's base.

"This is the Atlas District."

We're obviously out of place in our uniform grays. So many dress code violations litter the crowd that Cicero gives up pointing them out.

"We could live here?" Newton gapes at a woman in a cut-off gray sweater that shows her belly button.

"This is a slum." Cicero steps over a pile of trash in disgust and screws up her face at the stink.

"This is the only other neighborhood we'll be able to afford on our salary."

A man stumbles out of a bar and bumps into Cicero, hard, knocking the purse she's been clutching to the ground, spilling its contents all over the sidewalk. He mumbles something and starts to wobble off down the street. Another man rushes out of the bar after him, grabs him by the neck, and throws him against the wall. A crowd quickly gathers as the two drunks tussle, blocking us from leaving—the best we can do is to pick up most of Cicero's belongings off the sidewalk and attempt to dodge the brawlers and their swinging fists.

Two state police officers in heavy-looking helmets with dark face shields shove through the crowd. But rather than pulling the men apart, handcuffing them, and hauling them off in separate directions, the police begin beating the men with metal batons. The crowd falls silent as the men fight back, but their fists are no match for the police officers' riot gear. Soon, both men lay bleeding on the sidewalk, begging for mercy. But the blows keep coming.

A woman near the front of the crowd yells "enough!" to no effect. One of the police officers simply shoves her to the ground. A surge comes from the back of the crowd, as nearly the whole mob rushes forward, some pulling the two beaten men to safety, the rest falling on the police officers with beer bottles, fists, or whatever they have handy. The few civs who try to break up the fighting also fall victim to the mob's anger. We escape the fight, pushing our way out and across the street, but not before a stray elbow catches Newton on the jaw.

"You okay, son?" A man watching the action from a doorway across the street offers Newton the wet napkin from around his drink.

Newton wiggles his jaw around. "Just a little banged up."

The bystander sizes us up. "First time in the Atlas? Well, don't get the wrong idea. This is strange. Even for here. I was at the brawl over in the Pleasure District last week, and that didn't get near this bad. 'Course those officers were standing around when they got attacked—unprovoked. Probably put the whole force on the offense. With batons and all. And now, this! Rumor is the state's gonna arm 'em—bring back the guns."

The sound of approaching sirens proves to be the only thing that can break up the fighting. The crowd scatters before backup arrives.

Cicero starts back toward District B. "You two have fun living in this dump, but I'm moving into a nice, clean, safe apartment building in a neighborhood that isn't overrun by criminals, creeps, and garbage."

"You heard what that guy said. It's not usually this bad. And besides, I'll need a roommate." True. Although Cicero might not be the ideal choice . . .

Cicero turns around, the frown fading from her face. "Even after everything? Even after I turned you in for not making your bed last spring?"

"Absolutely." Come to think of it, there could be worse things than living with a neat-freak roommate who'll clean up after you.

"If you're really serious about it, let's look at an apartment tomorrow. During the day. Possibly with a police escort." Cicero turns to leave.

"Stop."

"I've already agreed to look at a place. I—"

"No, listen."

The sound is faint, garbled, muffled by the chatter of civs all around, but it's unmistakable. Singing.

"Where's it coming from?"

"There."

Newton points to an especially run-down, especially small black brick building. I head for the door, Newton right behind.

"What if it's NAA? We'll have to report it." Cicero hangs back at first but eventually follows us into the building.

Inside is a wall of warm, stuffy air and a blanket of darkness, pierced by a single spotlight pointed toward the front of the bar. The heat is body heat, generated by the hundred or so civs packed shoulder-to-shoulder in the cramped space, blocking the view as the crowd listens in silence to a man's voice as he sings a cappella—a slow tune . . . unfamiliar. It takes some shoving to get to the front, and just as the crowd parts enough, there's a break in the song, a pause before the next verse, and the face comes into view.

"Croon?!"

The man on stage is dressed like a civ—hair messed up, black and white striped socks pulled way up over his pants, sunglasses on, at night, indoors—but it's Euripides Croon, head of the WI's vocal instruction department, a teacher. Dr. Croon ignores the outburst and finishes the song. The crowd cheers as he steps away from the mic.

As the lights come up, Croon makes his way over, the look on his face something between a grimace and a scowl. He's never looked so furious.

"I think he may be injured." Newton backs toward the exit.

"What are you three doing here?"

"Well, we . . . I just . . . We could ask you the same thing." Cicero's face goes bright red. She isn't used to speaking out of turn. She should learn Darwin's Rule #1—Never Let 'Em See You Sweat.

"I am performing my duties as a licensed member of the WI. You three are breaking curfew."

Newton checks his watch and says a non-approved word. "We were just heading back to the dorm. Right, guys?"

"What was that song? Was it . . .?" It couldn't be NAA.

"It's an old song called 'Three is a Magic Number.' The education value is pretty low—simple multiplication—but vintage tunes are kind of my thing."

"I didn't know instructors performed, too."

"Most of us don't. I love standing in front of a crowd of civs. I know what they like, and they like me. So, what are you three doing here?"

"We're thinking about moving to the Atlas District."

Croon's expression softens. "Really? Living here . . . that's quite . . . adventurous of you." The instructor looks the three of us over as if he's never met us before. "Regardless, now's no time for apartment-hunting. The Atlas District can be dangerous at night."

"We know." Newton rubs his jaw.

"Well, what are you waiting for? Get back to the dorms. Now!"

We follow orders, heading back to the WI. No way is this goodbye for good, though—not after seeing how the neighborhood's lights, laughter, and colorful little buildings can make the rest of the city's towering gray skyrises seem flat.

2

A week's worth of packing, undone. Moving boxes emptied, my stuff's all over the dorm room floor when Cicero comes home just in time to witness my victory at the bottom of the last box.

"Found it! It's always the last place you look."

"Because once you find what you're looking for, you stop looking. What did you lose?"

"My library card." The small plastic card's raised numbers are just as clear as the day it was issued—barely used.

"The Private Library? That place is soooo expensive. Who owns it now?" Cicero sits down to help with the re-packing.

"MotoRama bought it right before they came out with their new hydrogen car. Don't you remember? Dr. Painter had to take a sabbatical from teaching so he could design the info-graphics—the whole building was covered in pictures of the car."

"Oh yeah—The Hydrogen Specialists. Why are you going there when you have access to the interweb for free?"

"The Private Library has some impossible-to-find stuff on their harddrives—old histories and songs."

"It's your money. Did you mean what you said last night? About us being roommates after integration? When can we go look at apartments?"

Can Cicero be trusted? One the one hand, there's the bed-making incident. On the other hand, there's . . . well, not much evidence to suggest my roommate can be trusted. Not that there's anything to hide. But a good friend keeps your secrets.

"I'll message you when I leave the library. What are you doing for the rest of the afternoon?"

"I'm seeing the new World War III history. With Newton."

"Really? The two of you?"

"Yeah. So?"

"Nothing. It sounds like—"

"It's not a date. Newton and I are friends. I was gonna invite you to come along, but you're headed off to waste your money at the Private Library."

"Okay, okay. Have fun on your not-a-date."

In the Pleasure District, between a brewpub and a mediaplex, there stands a big square building completely covered in a giant media screen. The Private Library. A red scooter rolls across the face of the building—an advertisement for MotoRama's new hydro-bike. A recording plays when the doors open.

"Welcome to the MotoRama Library, D.C. branch. Our featured collection today can be found on the bottom floor—a selection of MotoRama catalogs, specifications, and histories detailing the evolution of MotoRama's newest line of people movers—the Hydro Series . . ."

A media screen shows a detailed map of the library. The collection's organized chronologically, and the oldest section I can find is labeled 1960-2060, Pre-War, located in . . . the basement?

The place is deserted. Where are the couples watching histories on the compys near the window? And the guys checking out Motorama's latest inventions? A woman with short, white hair sits behind the front desk, watching a history on a celly and chewing away on some gum. The woman somehow manages to tear her eyes off the screen.

"May I help you?"

"Where is everybody?"

"Folks can't afford to read these days—not in this economy." She looks me up and down. "Payment up front."

14

"One hour. Can you show me where the pre-war collection is? The map says it's in the basement, but . . ."

Down some stairs, through a dimly lit hall ending in a thick, fancy wooden door (out of tempo with the open-air, glass-and-concrete plan of the rest of the library) lies what the neon sign above describes as the Atlas Wing. It's like a pre-war museum—wooden tables and chairs, hand-woven tapestries and rugs, glittering lamps and chandeliers, and shelves that rise to the ceiling, packed with books—actual made-of-paper books—locked safely behind glass. The only things that look current are the many stacks of hard drives and the compy on the large table in the center of the room.

The librarian lets herself out with a curt reminder, "one hour," and shuts the door behind her. A search for "NAA" in the compy brings up the usual results. *The WI: A History in Two Volumes* and the book from the other day's interweb surfing, simply called *NAA*. Useless.

The little room's strange, with its fuzzy tapestries and smooth wooden-backed chairs. You don't come across wood or hand-woven fabric much. There's even a big cushy velvet chair that could have doubled for a throne in a love history. What would it be like to live in a home surrounded by objects like these—old things that, unlike normal plastic, throwaway furniture, had been built to last, long ago—that someone else had once used and cared for? Living with someone else's memories sounds fine when you don't have many good ones of your own.

A closer look at the spines of the protected paper books shows that they're useless—*Cheese Through the Ages* and *Quantum Physics* and *The Consciousness Problem*. A handful of hard drives from a random shelf proves equally boring. It would've been a wasted trip if not for a single bulky old hard drive shoved way back on the bottom shelf. Somehow, it came into view: a mysteriously unzipped boot, a happenstance kneel, an offhand glance to the exact spot where it

15

had sat collecting dust for so long. The data on that drive wanted to be found.

Outside District B's leasing office, I meet Cicero and Newton, who brought along his friends and future roommates: Homer Thump, a chubby percussionist with glasses, and Franklin Keys, a piano player with his long dreadlocks and dark skin. The leasing agent is a middle-aged woman whose gray suit is so well-ironed it looks more like stiff paper than soycloth. None of us have lived anywhere but the dorms since we became initiates. We're used to twin beds, mini-fridges, and hallways that reek of rosemary-scented bleach. So the model unit, with its full-size kitchen, sectional sofa, and well-kept houseplants (that look fake) seems kind of like paradise.

"The basic unit is unfurnished," the leasing agent reminds us, "but the media screen is built into the wall. So, that'll be two basics . . . a two-bedroom for the girls and a three-bedroom for the guys." She pulls out a form on a clipboard and hands it to me. "Sign here."

Pen is put to page, but my hand refuses to write, to commit me to life inside a colorless cube. Fake plants are for people too lazy to keep real plants alive.

"I think we should look around some more. Weigh our choices."

The leasing agent laughs. "Not to be too blunt about it, dear, but aren't you all WI initiates? You don't really have a choice. Not with the amount of money you'll be making. Not unless . . ."

"Unless . . .?" Someone else has to say it.

"The Atlas District? You five wouldn't last a day over there."

"Clearly, you know nothing about us." But, no one follows me when I head for the door.

"Maybe she's right." Newton can't take his eyes off the giant media screen.

"Yesterday you were drooling all over the civilian girls we saw outside the Atlas Theater."

"And I also took a blow to the head, in case you've forgotten. But this place . . . Think of the football parties."

"Fine." The boys are out. I abandon them there in the model apartment. They aren't strong enough to handle the Atlas district if they can't even live without TV.

Cicero comes running up behind me. "Leaving without me?"

"I assumed you'd jumped ship, too."

"I promised we'd look for a place in the Atlas District. I keep my promises. Even when they're foolish and will probably end up getting both of us killed."

"Don't histories always start with one of the characters heading off on an adventure? Think of this as the start of our adventure."

A tingle shoots through my body—pre-show jitters? No. Jitters are for newbies, the inexperienced, the ill-prepared. This feeling's something else, something unfamiliar. Fear.

3.

"Lofts" are what they call dwelling units in the Atlas District. The move proves easy. When you don't have much of a past, there isn't much stuff to carry. *Loft.* It sounds so wrong. But it's totally legit (somehow), and no one at the WI seems to care. They give strange looks when they see the official forms with my new address written down, but no one says a word. Everything's fine.

Until it's not. Four in the morning, and there's a big recording session in . . . three hours, now. But sleep won't come. How can it, with the thump, thump, thump coming from upstairs? The noise starts at eleven and will surely die down by one or two. It doesn't. Three a.m.? Still thump, thump, thumping. What to do? This never would have happened in District B.

Cicero calls out from her bedroom. "Darwin?"

"Yeah?"

"You up?"

"Obviously."

"What should we do? Bang on the ceiling? Call the police?"

"I don't wanna be that girl—the nosy neighbor who calls the cops. I'll just go up there and ask them to turn it down."

Cicero meets me in the living room.

"You want me to come with you?"

"No." The move to the Atlas District was my idea. I'll handle the problems. "I'm taking my phone. Call if I'm not back in ten. If I don't answer, call the police."

The stairwell is surprisingly quiet considering how loud the noise is inside. An imaginary dry run of the conversation to come: Hi, I'm your new neighbor, Darwin. What a cute cat you have! I plan to toss it out a window if you don't SHUT UP.

Just outside the loft upstairs the thump, thump, thump is loud and clear. Music. Can't quite place the tune . . . A knock on the metal door gets no response. Another knock. Nothing. A hard lean on the buzzer produces a shrill *buzzzzz* from inside. The music stops. Footsteps approach the door. The deadbolt clicks, the latch turns, and the door opens.

"Yeah?"

A guy in a gray hooded sweatshirt opens the door a crack and pokes his head out. His eyes are red and puffy and mouth is tense, like he just ate a whole lemon. Aside from his scruffy-looking hair and that sour-puss face, he looks okay. You might even call him cute, if you're into the rude, inconsiderate type. His eyes are okay, nice actually, even if they are a little sad.

"Um . . . Sorry. I wasn't expecting . . . I'm your new neighbor. I moved in downstairs. Darwin." Instead of acknowledging the greeting and politely shaking the hand extended in front of him, he ignores it. "I was wondering if you could turn down the music? I've got work in the morning."

The neighbor says nothing—he just looks at me with those sad eyes. Hopefully, the blank stare means yes.

"Okay. Thanks." Problem solved, but . . . those bloodshot eyes. "Is everything—" Bam! The door slams. "Okay?"

Downstairs, Cicero's so panicked she drops her celly when the door opens.

"Well? Who is he? A hermit? A psychopath?"

"Shhh. Listen." No more thumping.

"Whoever thought silence could sound so sweet?" Cicero heads for her room.

"Cicero . . ."

"Hmm?" Cicero climbs into bed.

"Thanks for . . . I mean, I'm glad we moved in here together. I thought you'd drop out, for sure."

"I promised we'd move in together. I keep my promises. Even when they're foolish and will probably end up getting both of us killed."

"I think I heard . . . I'm not sure, but—"

"Let's talk tomorrow."

Sleep doesn't come easy, even without the noise. The thoughts just won't stop. A new place, a new life as an official, licensed member of the WI. Maybe having a real job will turn out to be more fun than school. Maybe this loft will turn out to be happier than the dorms. The upstairs neighbor—what was that about? Why did he stare like that? He could've been star-struck—maybe he recognized me from my album covers. It wouldn't be the first time a fan went speechless. What was he listening to?

Seven a.m. comes way too early. Cicero's still sleeping. No sign of life from upstairs. Figures. The civ keeps us up all night, and now he'll probably sleep the day away while everyone else trudges off to work.

The ereader stand on the corner outside the loft sells decent coffee—better than the goop in the WI breakroom, anyway. The first cup of coffee on the way to the first day of work as a grown-up. A moment to be savored, but Dr. Croon's picture is plastered on every ereader screen on the stand. He's the front page of *The Washington ePost*. The headline reads, "WI Official Outed in NAA Scandal." Unbelievable. Standing in the cold reading ereader screens on the way to your first day at work is no way to find out your mentor is a criminal.

Slouched in the back corner of the Metro train downtown is a much better way to lose your illusions. At least there's enough privacy to load up the *ePost* and clutch my ereader with sweaty hands for as long as I need to. The *ePost* is usually meticulous with its sources. It has to be, or it'll face charges of producing NAA for falsifying information. That's why there's no such thing as tabloids anymore—they flirt too closely with fiction. So, this bizarre article reads like nothing else. These are accusations, not facts.

The source says Croon's involved with "a music scene calling itself 'underground' and taking pride in breaking the rules governing art established by the Wagner Initiative." The story claims Croon writes and performs songs that have no educational value—songs meant simply to sound pretty or stir up emotions in the listener. A crime equaling treason, if true.

The WI headquarters buzzes like a hornet's nest. People walk through the halls quickly, not looking anyone in the eye, but watching everyone else just the same. And everyone's talking. The general idea: Croon's accuser is probably someone within the WI, so either one of us—Croon—is a criminal, or one of us—the unknown accuser—is a liar. The whole thing feels like something out of a history about spies—trust no one.

Outside the glass-walled recording studio we're scheduled to use, Newton's sitting in the hall, on the floor. The WI's belief that chairs and benches encourage laziness leads to a chronic shortage of seating.

"So, do you believe it? That Croon's been doing NAA?" Newton's never sounded so serious. "You saw him that night, up on stage. It was weird."

"Weird, but legal."

"Well somebody around here knows something."

"It seems . . . odd. Maybe. I don't know."

"What do you mean?"

"It's a crime to not report NAA right? If you knew something about Croon doing NAA, why not go straight to the police? Why would you risk getting yourself into trouble by talking to the press instead of the proper authorities?"

"It's faster—going straight to the paper and skipping the police."

"If they'd gone to the police, there would have to be an investigation."

"So, who knows how long that could take? Years, for all we know. Why run the ball when you can just aim for the end zone?"

"Someone wants Croon out of the WI. And fast. Why?"

A woman in a long gray dress rushes past, then stops and turns around. "You two. What are you doing? Recording sessions are cancelled for today. They've called an emergency hearing. All WI business is on hold." The woman resumes her rush down the hall.

The WI's biggest auditorium, a giant, domed hall, is full, every instructor here, along with most of the initiates. On stage sit several WI officials including Jefferson Planner, the state's most famous architect and current Artist General, the highest-ranking member of the WI in the country.

"If Planner's here . . ." The busy designer usually only comes to the WI for integration ceremonies. This is serious.

Planner wears a gray jacket emblazoned with the WI seal (two hands cradling a musical note), and he pulls at the collar as he picks up a gavel and bangs it on the desk three times. He smiles at the crowd.

"I hereby call this emergency disciplinary hearing to order. Dr. Euripides Croon, please approach the panel."

Croon steps from backstage looking more disheveled than usual. An anonymous "Boooooo!" comes from somewhere in the auditorium. Croon stands at a microphone next to the table, facing the audience.

"Dr. Croon . . ." Planner pauses and shuffles through some papers on the table. "Excuse me."

Newton nudges me. "What's he doing?"

The girl sitting in front of us turns around—she's one of the acting kids. "He's got a script up there to follow, I'll bet. No way he's got this ceremony memorized. A disciplinary hearing hasn't happened in ages—decades."

Planner puts on a pair of glasses and begins to read from a sheet in front of him (breaking Darwin's Rule #9—Memorize Your Lines). By now the crowd is standing-room-only.

"Dr. Euripides Croon, the purpose of this disciplinary hearing is two-fold. First, we must inform you that you are under investigation for criminal activities including violations of the Wagner Initiative. After this hearing is over, you will be taken into police custody. Do you understand?"

Croon says nothing. He stares at the mic, silent.

"Second, we must inform you that as of today, pending a verdict on the charges against you, you are hereby stripped of all your duties in relation to the WI including performances and providing instruction to WI initiates. Do you understand?"

Croon stands at the microphone, silent. Why isn't he saying anything?

"If you are found not guilty of the charges alleged against you, an additional hearing will be called to determine whether you may be reinstated as a member of the WI. Do you understand?"

Croon says nothing. The crowd begins to whisper.

"This hearing is adjourned. Please take the accused into custody."

Planner bangs the gavel once. A handful of police officers approach Croon, and he lets himself be handcuffed and led off stage. Planner and the rest of the high-ups follow. The audience files out the auditorium.

Croon didn't defend himself. Was it because there's some truth to the accusations? Or because defending himself won't make a difference?

In one of the histories that Cicero and I watched a lot in the dorms, the men of a pre-war city accuse women of being witches. To find out if a woman was a witch, they tied huge stones to her feet and threw her into a river. If she drowned and died, they knew she was human after all. If she somehow survived and lived—they took this as proof of magic and burned her at the stake. After a long, late-night discussion over popsoy, it was decided that the witch trials weren't really about witches at all. The trials were about using fear to gain power—the men thought women's fear of being pronounced a witch would make them easier to control. Women who disobeyed their husbands were witches, outcasts who deserved to be drowned or burned at the stake.

Croon's arrest is different, though. A power play can't be behind it. We've moved past accusing people of witchcraft, haven't we?

4.

A chance finally comes to download the files from the library. They read like news stories, but they're from a weird source— *Rolling Stone* magazine. And the photos—the people look like they stepped right out of a Halloween party—freakish makeup and clothes (on some of them; others are nearly naked). The stories outline the exploits of musicians and other artists from the mid-1900s until the late 21st century, when the Wagner Initiative began. The detailed chronicles of drug-crime, sex-crime, gun-crime—these artists did it all, and everyone knew about it. No wonder this stuff is banned.

Thankfully, the NAA articles are short. They're read and deleted before Cicero, fresh out of the shower, a towel wrapped around her head, walks through the living room.

"You've heard."

"Croon's all over the news." Cicero starts some coffee. "I found something for you. By the door."

Between Croon's disciplinary hearing and the library texts, it would seem there's no way this day could get stranger. The sheet of paper, folded in half, with *Darwin* written on it proves otherwise. It's a flyer, hand-drawn, advertising "Irregular Records." It takes a minute (and some helpfully drawn musical notes) to figure out that the word *records* means *media*. A new media store.

Cicero looks up from the stove. "What is it?"

"A flier for a media store."

"Who left it? Let me see. The address is in the Business District, but I don't remember a media store being there."

"Maybe it just opened."

"A 'record' store . . ."

"New slang or something, I guess."

"You know what I think this is?"

"You think it's a store that sells NAA."

"And I think that boy upstairs left it for you. What have you gotten yourself into?"

The neighbor doesn't say a word when we're face-to-face, but then there's this note. He blasts music at four in the morning, but turns it down without protest when a stranger asks him to. What's going on?

"I'm not sure, but I have a feeling it's gonna be interesting."

The Business District, home to most of D.C.'s stores, banks and corporation headquarters, attacks all five senses. There's hardly ever a reason to come into this part of the city—in fact, most locals avoid the neighborhood altogether. The constant flow of tourists, of civs shouting from storefronts, shoving flyers in your face, attacking you with a spritz of too-sweet perfume . . . The endless drone of cars, honking horns, dozens of video billboards blaring away, hawking supermarkets, banks, sports drinks with added electrolytes . . . Seems like they should've shut the whole district down by now.

The mannequins in store windows heavily bundled against the fake snow inside make my thin jacket seem even more inadequate against high winds and slushy puddles. Luckily, the address on the flyer is easy to find. It's a giant, gray, windowless cube. The Business District is filled with giant, gray, windowless cubes, but this building lacks signage—no media screen wrapped around it, no video showing the happy, productive workers inside, not even a set of understated neon lettering, like on the state buildings on Government Street. Weirder: The slab of concrete making up the building's front side extends all the way to the ground. No door.

But there's a narrow alley hiding between this building and the next. And a sign, like the ones used near construction sites, reads DETOUR and points down the alley. A detour sign isn't strange in a city like D.C., where buildings and roads constantly get demolished and rebuilt, but this sign seems out of place. Where is the equipment? The workers? Where's any sign of construction?

Instinct pushes me down the alley. The Business District's constant whine fades to a dull roar. On either side, the concrete buildings rise high, leaving only a small rectangle of gray sky visible above, turning the alley into a long, dark tunnel. It brings back old memories of sneaking out at night to ramble through the WI's dark, deserted hallways. The hall outside the records room was a favorite, dark place to sit for hours, cross-legged on the floor, wondering if my permanent record, locked inside that room, held clues about my parents, how I ended up a ward of the state, and whether I'd ever be free, not knowing back then that WI headquarters functioned like a boarding school that you leave when you turn 16, and that most initiates actually *did* see their parents from time to time. Back then, the place was nothing more than a series of dark halls and locked doors—a prison.

The alley ends in a fenced-in area behind the unnamed building. On a heavy-looking door with no window hangs a sign that reads, "Slide Deliveries Under Door." Nothing else. No one answers a knock at the door, which refuses to budge. Improvising seems like the way to go, so I pull the flier out of my bag and slide the folded piece of paper under the door. Worth a shot. The lock clicks and the door opens a crack. Looking out at me are those two sad, mysterious eyes from the night before.

So, the upstairs neighbor *did* leave the note. "Wasn't sure you'd show."

"I wasn't either."

The boy shuts the door behind us, and locks it. We stand on the landing of a staircase that leads up into the giant cube and down to the basement. We head down. The basement is a small yellow room that smells of mildew and is crammed with tables of bins full of media drives. Pictures like the ones in *Rolling Stone* cover the walls and ceiling. The whole place is plastered with musicians in tight, ripped, colorful outfits or wearing nothing at all. Even crazier, pieces of black plastic shaped like flat donuts hang on the walls. An obsolete type of music media—illegal because the only thing ever printed on them was NAA. Cicero was right about what this store has to offer.

Heart racing, my body is ready to flee, to run home and forget this place and this boy. But, no. You don't go this far just to turn back.

"Welcome to Irregular Records." He seems a lot happier today than last time we spoke—well, one of us spoke.

"What is this place?"

"I think you know." He pulls out a metal detector wand and waves it in front of my body. "Checking for hidden recording devices. We're on a tight security lockdown."

He glances at a bank of small media screens showing feeds from what must be hidden cameras placed in front of the building, in the alley, and on the landing of the stairs. Tight security, indeed.

"We?" No one else is in the tiny store. "Who are you? Why did you want me to come here?"

"Don't panic." He offers his hand. "I'm Brax. And this is the reason I wanted you to come here."

He places a media-drive in my hand. It's labeled "Nursery Rhymes."

"People used to call these mix-tapes. Listen to it alone. It'll blow your mind apart."

"Is it . . . NAA?"

With all that research on Non-Approved Art, it should have been obvious that some of it would wind up in my hands. The drive, no bigger than my little finger, no heavier than a tube of lip-gloss, is without a doubt the most powerful, most dangerous thing I've ever touched.

"Why me? Don't you know who I work for?"

"Everyone in the Atlas District knows that you and your roommate are newly integrated WI personnel. Lots of people—lucky for you, not the wrong people, yet—also know that you've been poking your head down some holes that could be hazardous to your health. You should try to be a little more discreet."

"How . . .? Oh. The Private Library." Of course they'd keep records of the files accessed.

"Jackpot." Brax glances at the alley cam as a figure moves across the screen. Then, on the landing cam, a piece of paper slides under the door. "Be right back. Make yourself at home."

A closer look at the store only reveals more of the same: illegal paraphernalia everywhere. In the center, a long bin displays media drives labeled with nonsense words and phrases like "Beatles" and "Wu-Tang Clan." Must be some kind of code.

Brax rushes back in the door. "Come on," he says, note in hand. "Let's go."

"What's wrong?" If I get caught here . . .

"Closing for the day. No big deal."

As we make it to the landing, a series of men in gray jumpsuits carrying boxes and trash bins pass by. When we reach the end of the alley, Brax takes off down the street without saying goodbye. First impressions are always right—he's still rude and inconsiderate.

Once again the Metro provides a safe haven for world-changing events. State-of-the-art headphones are made to play songs about traffic safety and proper hygiene, but they work just as well for a media drive filled with illegal music. The first song is dissonant, the singer's voice scratchy like maybe she's overworked it, the recording quality's terrible, and the lyrics . . . drugs and sex and the merits of doing nothing all day long. The next song seems to be about love—and it starts with a guitar riff that would make Newton drool. The other people on the train stand shuffling feet in worn-out sneakers, sit clutching grocery bags full of a week's shopping, frown chatting with co-workers about today's work and tomorrow's work while a single person sits among them, secretly breaking away from her boring old gray life, finally living in color.

While the music plays, the Atlas District stop comes and goes, and I don't even notice. At the next stop, standing on the platform, waiting to catch a train going back in the opposite direction, shaking off the effects isn't easy. Brax's music doesn't have any lessons to teach, but more important—more dangerous—is the way it made me *feel*. It's like inventing the light bulb, discovering fire, setting foot on dry land, never to look back at the ocean.

Someone else has to know. Telling anyone will be a risk—the biggest risk ever, but Newton and Cicero have to know. Can they be trusted? Croon probably trusted the person who turned him in. But this isn't like Croon. This isn't making NAA—it's just listening a little, dabbling. Nothing to be ashamed of.

The way Newton and Cicero stare only makes telling them harder. It's been a week since the trip to Irregular Records, since I told Cicero it was a regular media store. Another lie.

"I . . . don't know how to say this. It's kind of shocking."

"You're pregnant!" Newton says it, then blushes.

Cicero punches him in the arm. "Blurt it out."

How to explain? Say it was a transcendental experience on the Metro? They wouldn't understand. Better to let them hear for themselves. I plug the media drive Brax gave me into a set of speakers. The music starts. Now it's time for Cicero and Newton to react.

As soon as the lyrics come on (spoken-word poetry about having lots of money and partying in someplace called the "VIP"), Cicero stands up and, without saying a word, walks out the door. Newton sits there, alternately laughing, staring slack-jawed, and shaking his head.

"What the . . .? How did you? I . . . You're crazy."

"What's your opinion? Of the music. Not my sanity or lack thereof."

"It's different. Frantic. Happy. Utterly pointless. Fantastic."

"Right? Why aren't we writing music like this?"

"Because we don't live in the 1900s." Newton bops his head to the beat. "And because we don't want to go to jail."

"We could do it, though. The two of us—we have the talent. And there's nothing wrong with the music."

"Darwin, the guy in that song listed about a hundred different crimes."

"So? Talking about crimes isn't the same as committing them, is it?"

"We're committing a crime by listening to this."

"I know. Wanna hear more?"

"Absolutely."

5.

The music's been on repeat for seven days straight—a soundtrack to the weirdest week ever. At home, Cicero refuses to talk, apart from single-syllable replies to direct questions. At work, there's no news of Croon other than the official press conference given by the WI announcing the charges brought against him. Since the roomie's become an expert at the silent treatment, Newton plays sidekick on a fact-finding mission at the D.C. jail— the biggest building in the Pleasure District. Unlike prisons in history films, all concrete and barbed wire, the present-day D.C. jail is a tower made of floor-to-ceiling windows (five-inch-thick bulletproof glass), allowing views both in and out, reminding those on the outside of the consequences of breaking the law and those on the inside of the pleasures their crimes have cost them. From the ground, you can see inmates in gray jumpsuits on the first few floors pacing back in forth in their cells, sitting on their beds, or staring out at the city below.

They make it easy to find inmates to visit—only being able to talk to friends and family through a glass wall is another crime deterrent. The courtesy compy at the reception desk lists Croon's name and cell assignment on the inmate roster. The glass-walled elevator glides up several floors and we walk the halls, passing inmate after inmate, until there's Croon sitting in his cell, staring at the wall, his eyes unfocused, his usually neat beard untrimmed. He looks . . . wrong.

It's suddenly too hot, and this place has the same rosemary-bleach stink as the WI. The smell makes my lunch threaten to come up. Stripping off my scarf and unzipping my jacket don't help. Newton puts a hand on my shoulder and the panic fades—a little.

Newton speaks into the intercom on the wall. "Dr. Croon, we're here to . . ."

"We're here to find out the truth, I guess."

Croon jumps as if he's only just noticed the two people standing no more than five feet away from him. "What do you want to know?"

"Why are you in here?"

"On charges associated with NAA."

"What, exactly, are the charges?"

"I don't know."

"Who accused you? Why aren't you out on bail? Do you have a lawyer?"

My hands busy themselves tying my scarf into knots. Otherwise they'd be shaking. After years of performing, nerves shouldn't be a problem, but this place . . .

"A state-appointed lawyer has advised me that the best way to handle the situation is to be as cooperative as possible, and that means showing I intend to serve my time willingly if I'm found guilty. Listen, kids, you shouldn't have come to see me. I'm glad you did—I appreciate the company—but there's no point in . . . getting yourselves involved."

"But you're innocent."

"It's not that simple. Sometimes doing what you know is right means doing what the rest of the world thinks is wrong."

An alarm signals the end of visiting hours, and the intercom automatically switches off. Croon gives a limp wave goodbye and turns away, looking out the window, down at the swarm of people enjoying themselves on the streets below.

Against all odds, Cicero's given up the silent treatment by the time the failed prison reconnaissance mission is over. In fact, the usually grim-faced writer's all smiles. Something must be wrong.

"I wasn't sure what time you'd be home. We have a guest."

Is this a police inquisition or party? A strange woman sits on the couch with her hands folded in her lap. The woman looks about Croon's age, wears a wrinkled gray dress and has brown, freckled skin and messy curls—like mine.

"Meet Lucy. Your mother."

"I'm sorry, what?"

Her face looks familiar, but there's no real recognition there. We may as well be strangers. We *are* strangers.

"How did you . . .?"

"Once I knew that you were sixteen and out of that place, I hired an investigator to find you. I wasn't sure you'd want to meet me, so . . ."

"So she talked to me first, and I asked her to come. She doesn't live too far from here—few blocks away, a nice two-bedroom in District B."

"I keep your room the way it was the day they took you away."

The memory starts to come back—holding on to this woman with one hand, a stuffed bear with the other. This *is* her. She was there when they took me.

"Why did you let them?"

"I was scared. I didn't want any trouble. You were singing a song you made up about your stuffed animals—I couldn't get you to stop. Your father had just . . . he was gone. I didn't know what else to do. I had to let them take you. And music is your calling, isn't it? It's what you love?"

A childhood taken away because of a song about toys. It might be funny if it wasn't so tragic. Snatches of the tune come back—a simple four-note melody—and a memory follows with it: humming the song as a WI recruitment officer carries me out the door.

"I thought maybe your mother could talk some sense into you. About the big news you had the other day." Cicero nods her head toward my speakers.

"Listen, girls, if you're mixed up in something dangerous, I know someone who might be able to help you." Lucy fishes a business card out of her purse and hands it to me. Then, she heads for the door. "Darwin . . . Darwin—the name we gave you was Melody—I hope one day we can be friends."

And she's gone, no tear-filled apology, no hug, not even a "How's life treating you?" Things never go the way you imagine them.

The business card is printed with a phone number, but no name above it, only a series of letters: BCA, VIII. The first thing my mother has bothered to give me in 13 years.

Cicero sits down next to me. "Listen, if I shouldn't have told her to come . . ."

"What's yours like?"

"My mom?"

"Yeah. I mean—you don't have to talk about her if you don't want to."

"She's fine. My dad, too. You've heard all my stories about what they were like before I joined the WI."

"What are they like now that you're out on your own?"

"Honestly? We don't know each other anymore, really. Yeah, I spent the first ten years of my life with them, but . . . Seems like all the important stuff happened at the WI. My braces—government issue. My first bra—government issue. My parents want me to move back in."

"Are you?"

"And give all this up? Not a chance. I'm sorry if—"

"You wanted her to help me come to my senses."

"We could get into a lot of trouble."

"We? So, you liked what you heard?"

"I've got something to show you." Cicero disappears into her room and comes out carrying a paper book with worn edges and bookmarks sticking out from all sides. "'I am no bird; and no net ensnares me.' It's from the book."

The pages are yellowed and lined with hand-written notes. Passages are underlined and highlighted. This is no history book. Surprise, surprise, Miss Follow-the-Rules has been hiding a novel.

"I found it in the Private Library, years ago. Well—not exactly *in* the library so much as in a pile on the side of the building waiting to be recycled. I didn't know the PL even had paper books. I picked it up and read that line, and I had to take it. I read it over and over, wishing I could write that way, and hating myself for wishing it."

"That's why you walked out when I played the music."

"I kept that book hidden for so long, and then to hear you play that . . . I was ashamed."

"Are you willing to consider the possibility that music—and books—that break the rules of the Wagner Initiative aren't inherently evil?"

"I'm willing to consider it."

"Then listen to this."

Heavy piano chords ring out, one after another, followed by a delicate melody. It's classified as classical music. Cicero won't realize—she's a writing student, after all—but the melody is the first one they teach you to sing at the WI. The instructors probably have no clue that this bit of NAA, this relic, is the foundation of all of their musical training. Darwin's Rule #14—There Are No New Ideas.

"It's beautiful. Like swimming through the sky." Cicero closes her eyes and listens. "Like a dream."

"No." It's better than that. "It's like waking up."

6.

A folded piece of paper slides under the door. Cicero puts down her novel (she's decided to read it again, in celebration), gets up, and hands the piece of paper over. A note from Brax. Has the weirdo never heard of a phone? *Meet at my loft 8 tonight. Bring your friends. Wear party clothes.*

By the time eight rolls around, a week's pay and the entire afternoon have been spent in the Business District. A party is the perfect excuse to buy new clothes. Cicero quickly throws on the most festive outfit in her closet—a ruffled gray dress with gray tights—and spends the rest of the day watching me pull out every pair of brightly colored socks I own. I've always wanted to dress this way. I just never had the chance.

Dressed and standing together on the landing outside Brax's door, Newton, Cicero, and I must look quite the trio—Cicero in her pretty gray dress, Newton in a gray suit ("You clean up nice," Cicero says. "Who knew?"), and me in a gray sequined tutu with my bright purple socks pulled up as far as they can go.

Brax opens the door. "Welcome to my humble abode. Let me grab some stuff, and then we'll go."

Sporting a long gray trench coat that balloons out behind him, our upstairs neighbor speeds through his mostly bare loft (a mattress in the corner, a bean-bag chair, and a media screen), opening drawers and cabinets and pulling out keys, a wallet, and three media-drives. As he leads us out the door, he hands one media-drive to each of us.

"Some more tunes to enjoy."

An hour-long train ride leads to a part of D.C. entirely new. Street after street of nearly identical concrete cube houses sprawl out in every direction, each one placed behind a plot of dead grass, most of them surrounded by waist-high iron fences.

"Where are we? Who lives way out here?"

"Families, mostly." Brax points to the houses lining each side of the street. "People trying to get away from the city, the fighting. You've seen it. People in D.C. are angry at the state."

It's hard to imagine a family living in one of these little, lonely houses, kids playing on the grass, mom reading in an armchair, dad grilling on the deck. The only image that comes to mind is an old, gray hermit, pants pulled up to his neck, surrounded by books and newspapers, living by himself—lots of old, gray hermits actually, one hermit in each house, together out here, living all alone.

"But why would people be mad at the state?" Newton delivers the question like a joke, but no one laughs.

"The dress codes and the WI. Older folks say the state has always been controlling, but . . . it's like they've taken away the parts of us that make us *us*. Some people have started fighting back. Others are scared. I don't blame them. I do blame them for moving all the way out here—instead of trying to make the problem better, they're running away from it. Sooner or later, it's bound to catch up. Anyway, you've never left the city?"

"Why would we?"

"Fair enough. But now you have a reason."

A bowling alley sits on the outskirts of the neighborhood, lit up with so many neon signs that a green halo surrounds the building. A few people head inside—a family or two with small children. Bowling's a dying pastime. Most hobbies have gone the way of other NAA—knitting and needlepoint were outlawed. Gambling, too, because people get addicted to winning and depressed when they lose. Emotional highs and lows ruin productivity. The only really government-approved hobby is sports. Sports allow you to show off your hard work and skill—the person or team that practices more wins. (SFL games don't count). Bowling technically counts as a sport, but it's not popular—it moves slowly, and it lacks chances for the bowler to show off. Basically, it's boring. The inside of the bowling alley, though, is almost as overwhelming as the Business District, with its bright lights, green and gold swirl carpet, and loud music.

Newton yells over the music. "Overcompensating with all this, aren't they?"

"Trying to lure people in, I think." Cicero examines a pamphlet about bowling's health benefits. "It would help if you could do something here other than bowl."

"That's the plan." Brax leads us past the bowling shoe station, giving the attendant a nod, and over to a door guarded by a large bald man.

"Private party," says the bouncer.

"'Scuse me while I kiss the sky."

The bouncer opens the door. Brax leads the way down a flight of stairs.

"We use basements, alleyways, attics. Anyplace we can get a little bit of privacy. The password and location change every week. If you're invited, we send you the phrase and place."

"We?"

Brax opens the door at the bottom of the stairs to a . . . the best word to use is *circus*. But unlike the circuses in history texts, this one has no elephants, and the action takes place inside a dingy basement instead of a red and blue striped tent. Fire-breathers in leather bikinis spew columns of flame that lick the ceiling. Jugglers in purple and green suspenders toss knives back and forth at breakneck speed. Break-dancers in blue jeans boogie and spin on pieces of cardboard taped to the floor, and a guy in a prison jumpsuit spray-paints yellow flowers onto a wall that has already been painted a hundred times over. A man in a black tuxedo stands in the center of it all, reciting a monologue that no one can hear over the music.

Music! In the far corner, on a tiny stage, a band, a group of teenage boys in flannel shirts and blue jeans, plays live, completely illegal, written-by-civilians, terrible-from-atechnical-standpoint-but-not-totally-unpleasant, non-approved music.

Brax takes off his gray trench coat and throws it on top of a stack of other trench coats piled in the corner, exposing his bright blue suit underneath. "What do you think?"

"Nice suit." Newton looks down at his own plain gray suit with a frown.

"Thanks. I meant, what do you think of the party?"

"Wild." Unbelievable, the way the band's singer screams into the microphone.

"Twisted." Newton ogles a girl in a leopard-print leotard as she contorts her body into impossible positions.

Cicero spots a guy sitting in the corner and writing furiously in a notebook. "I'll catch up with you later."

She heads straight for him. The young writer looks up and gestures for her to sit on the floor next to him.

"Me too." Newton goes to talk to a group of girls painting each other's faces to look like cats and dogs.

A small crowd of people is gathered to watch the band, some dancing, some jumping up and down in time with the beat, and others standing still, listening. Without knowing too much about NAA, it's still easy to notice how different this music is from the illegal music on my media drive. This band, their music is . . . bad. Obviously, none of the people on stage have any formal musical training (so much for Darwin's Rule #4—Practice, Practice, Practice). The singer can barely carry a tune, the drummer rushes the song, and the guitar player misses note after note. Their instruments look homemade or stolen from a landfill.

"Isn't it great?"

Brax is grinning like it's the best thing he's ever heard. The band's energy *is* contagious. And the chorus is easy to memorize. Brax bobs his head and sways to the beat. My body, on the other hand, has no clue how to move.

"I've never danced before."

"What?!"

"I'm not a trained dancer, so . . . I mean, you're not supposed to."

Brax throws his hands in the air and waves them (like he doesn't care). "Like this." He moves his head back and forth like a chicken and stomps his feet on the ground. "Like this."

The band starts a down-tempo song. Brax pulls me close, and puts his hands on my hips. This whole night is delirious—awkward, funny, awesome, and frightening. Dancing for the first time, surrounded by the energy of a hundred artists doing what they love. And Brax . . .

"So why were you crying the night we met, when I came up to ask you to turn down the music?"

"I wasn't crying."

"Your eyes were red and you looked like a sad puppy."

"I wasn't crying. I was . . . upset. D.C. had lost and—"

"You were crying over a football game?"

"No, I . . . Well, yes, but . . . We were having such a good season . . . I'm sure you cry over all those sappy histories you watch." Brax puts a falsetto, making fun of my voice. "Oh, Antony and Cleopatra, the rich and the powerful, how absolutely tragic," he says. "I bet you've never even seen a real movie, have you? Girl, you don't know what you're missing. Samurai fights, explosions, sex scenes. I can't wait to show you. Dinosaurs, flying robots, talking chimpanzees—"

He keeps talking, but between the music and my heart beating like a drum, paying attention is out of the question. Everything about tonight is overwhelming. And here's this rebel taking a huge risk bringing me and my friends, WI members, into his world. How does he know we won't turn him in? He doesn't. He's willing to sacrifice his safety for the greater good.

He starts to ask me a question, but before he's finished, my lips are on his. The kiss is nothing like the ones in love histories. The actors playing Antony and Cleopatra have to fake it. This is real: soft, warm, and awkward. We're both sweaty from dancing and we probably look like two wet dogs attempting to eat each other, but caring about looks right now is out of the question. Right now, it's just me and him. Us.

"What was that for? I mean—" The surprise on Brax's face is, well, surprising. Hasn't he been flirting this whole time?

"I dunno. It just . . . felt good." Good, great, like a Metro train careening through my head . . .

Brax smiles. "Now you're thinking like a rebel."

"Is that a compliment or an accusation?"

He doesn't answer. I don't care.

7.

Weeks pass and the underground NAA scene gradually reveals its depths. With the help of a rogue seamstress, my illegal clothing collection grows from a single rainbow-colored sock drawer to an entire dresser filled with a brightly colored wardrobe that would make an old-timey clown jealous. There are dance parties, underground plays, and poetry slams. And late night movie screenings with Brax that tend to devolve into snuggling on the couch in his loft . . .

But diving deeper into the world of NAA means opening up to a bunch of strangers. Each new friend is also a possible enemy. There's a chance that, hiding behind every new face is the backstabber who betrayed Croon and turned him over to the state. And an important question still hasn't been answered.

"What's the big deal?" The street outside the Atlas Theatre is unusually crowded for such a cold afternoon, making it hard to keep up with Brax as we step out of a history screening into the flow of people on the sidewalk. "I see these people everywhere. Over there—the guy with the soydog cart. I recognize him. He swallows swords, right? And the girl who scanned our tickets at the theater, she's a mime. But, out here, in the light of day, they're the same as all the other civs."

"Not really." Even though Brax faces straight ahead instead of looking my way, there's no mistaking an edge in his voice that's never been there before.

"In the ways that matter to the state, they are. *We* are. We pay taxes. We're no more likely to be criminals than anyone else."

"We *are* criminals. Your question is why are certain types of art illegal? My answer is I don't know. Maybe someone out there knows, but I can guarantee it's not the police enforcing the laws or even the bigwigs at the WI."

"Then, who?"

"What about that teacher of yours that got locked up?"

"Croon?"

"You said he didn't defend himself when they accused him. Don't you think it's possible he knows more than he's saying?"

Croon did seem like he was holding something back during that visit to the jail. But that was before, when NAA was just something imaginary, a ghost story told to keep frightened civs in line. Now that it's real . . .

"Let's go see him."

It's about an hour before the end of visiting hours at the jail—plenty of time to talk. Once again the walk up to Croon's cell takes us past the inmates staring down at the Pleasure District's happy crowds. The place is designed to provoke sadness and dread. And the dread increases when it becomes clear that the cell where the vocal instructor is supposed to be sits empty.

"Maybe he got moved." Brax walks up and down the hallway, looking into the other cells.

A check of the compy downstairs reveals that Croon's been released, but it's hard to tell whether that's good news or bad. It's hard to imagine a fate worse than rotting away in this sterile jail.

"Like transferred to another jail?" Brax leans in close over my shoulder to read the screen.

"Doesn't say."

Maybe this is for the best. Why is Brax so interested in Croon, anyway?

He's is quiet the whole way back to the Atlas district, but it's obvious Brax has something to say. As we approach the loft building, he finally comes out with it.

"I'm leaving for a little while."

"Where are you going?"

"It's kind of a business trip."

"You never did tell me who you work for . . ."

"I work for Atlas . . . I'll only be gone a couple days."

Brax holds the door as we go inside. We pause in the tight, cramped, musty lobby—not exactly ideal for having what might turn out to be a very important conversation. It may have only been a few weeks since that first kiss but since then he's done so much, told me so much about Non-Approved Art . . . there's no telling what the price will be. Nothing in life is free—not even information. Not even from your not-quite-but-almost boyfriend.

"Tell me what you're doing. Don't you trust me?"

"Atlas is a big name in this city. He has big secrets."

"And you have to keep those secrets for him?"

"Listen, you work on figuring out what happened to your Professor Croon, and when I get back we'll—"

"Sure. Yeah, see you when you get back." The nerve! He's still talking even after I've already rushed upstairs and slammed the door.

"Darwin!"

Looking at the guy who's been lying to me since we met would only make things worse, so there's no point opening the door and attempting to continue this conversation. Instead, it's time to put on some music and turn it up loud. Once Brax has given up banging on the door, the music can go away. What's that saying? Silence is golden. Listening to absolutely nothing at all is better than listening to his lies. All this time and he couldn't talk about working for Atlas. What else is he hiding?

In the short time since the fight my tablet is already covered in words like "jerk," "betrayal," and "red flag." My hands don't like to be idle, so they roam over the touchscreen, typing random words and phrases, but as the afternoon turns into night, the bits and pieces become poetry—

lyrics. A tune begins to form, music notes pasted at the top of the screen. The more notes and lyrics appear, the more my worries about Brax and Croon slip away. Music fills my head, leaving no room to care about how right now, doing what I'm doing makes me an outlaw.

From my second-story window, it's easy to watch without being seen as Brax drives away on his hydrobike, a duffel bag strapped to his back. Maybe yesterday's freak-out was an overreaction . . .

No. Brax is the one being strange. He's got something to hide. That much is clear. He doesn't want to tell his whole life story. Maybe that's fair—we barely know each other. He doesn't have to tell me anything. But it's hard not to think the secrecy is a sign that Brax is dangerous. He's gone for now, and that's reason enough not to think of him—to try really hard and focus on anything but him.

Thankfully, I've got lyrics to re-read. Over coffee and toast in the morning, the writing from last night doesn't seem quite right. The wording is off.

Cicero comes out of her bedroom and pours herself a cup of coffee, too. "Whatcha working on?"

"Lyrics."

"I take it this isn't official WI business, since I'm the only one in this household who is licensed to write lyrics. Mind if I have a look? Gimme."

Cicero deletes words, phrases, and entire lines.

"Hey!" I'm no Cicero, but those lyrics were pretty good.

"Trust me," Cicero says, still typing. "I know what I'm doing." She hands the notebook back to me.

The lyrics, her changes included, are good—really good.

"Sitting on a skyrise / gray days dance before my eyes. / You rush in, a burning child / catch fire to a world defiled . . ."

"So what are you planning to do with that?"

"What do you mean?"

"At work, when I write song lyrics, I send them to someone like you and then you sing them. Granted, our songs are usually about crosswalk safety . . . You should perform it."

Performing in front of a crowd of screaming rebels hasn't been a lifelong fantasy like, say, singing on a history soundtrack, but performing live does give a certain rush that recording in a studio can't match. But this is different.

"You're saying we should start a band."

"We?"

"You're the one who wrote the killer lyrics. I'm just a voice. And it was your idea to perform."

"How am I supposed to perform?" Cicero grabs the notebook back and scribbles more changes to the lyrics.

"You'll play tambourine or something."

"We could get Newton to play guitar."

"And his buddies Homer and Franklin on drums and keyboard."

"We could be good. Like, really good. Has a WI-trained performer ever gone underground? Other than maybe Croon?"

"Speaking of Croon—he's gone. We went to the jail last night to visit him. He wasn't there."

"That's because he's out. Didn't you see the news? Some unnamed benefactor posted his bail and paid for him to get a real lawyer. He hasn't been seen since his release. Keeping a low profile, I guess."

"Unnamed benefactor, huh?" Instantly, the business card my mother gave me comes to mind. "Remind me to thank her for this." Unfortunately, there's no answer at the phone number on the card. No voicemail. Endless ringing.

Cicero picks up the card and reads. "BCA, VIII . . . B.C. Atlas, the 8th? Your mother knows Atlas?"

"Or has at least met him. Maybe I should thank her sooner rather than later."

Lucy—or Mom, as awkward as calling her that feels—looks uneasy in this small café in the Atlas District. She nervously clutches a cup of steaming tea and stares out the window as we chat, like she's waiting for someone to pass by. But no one passes by. The place, with its cozy armchairs and soft lighting, is tucked away down a dead-end street, and the only people who stop in are regulars. There's always someone you know here, which takes me back to that feeling of being part of a community that's the one (and only) thing to miss about living in the WI dorms.

The server (a rebel who looks familiar even though she hides her pink mohawk under a wig) brings out the food, and there's small talk. My mother has no idea what her daughter's been up to these last thirteen years—the sock obsession, the Grammy for that toothbrush PSA in the lesser-known Best Female Vocal—Medical and Personal Hygiene category. She talks about her work in the state information retrieval office—pretty boring stuff, but she knows a lot about the legal system.

"And my father? Tell me about him."

"Your dad was WI, like you. A horn player. When you were born, all he could talk about was whether the two of you might get to record a song together one day. He knew he wasn't supposed to, but he sang to you. One day he went to work and never came back. The paperwork says he fell off a ship during a routine dedication ceremony—that they tried to rescue him, but the life preserver failed to deploy. By the time a drummer who knew how to swim jumped in after him, it was too late. They never found him."

"I'm so sorry." Cicero hands Lucy a spare napkin.

"But they didn't use horns for dedication ceremonies back then. They used strings. I know there's no way your father should have been on that boat."

To gain a father and lose him in the space of a single conversation—brutal. But it doesn't hurt like it should. It's not quite real. His disappearance is just another piece in a puzzle that's turning out to be even more complicated than it seems.

"This business card you gave me with Atlas's initials on it. Why is he so important?"

"He's the CEO of Atlas Realty, which owns the entire Atlas district."

"That explains the statue."

"The company has holdings throughout the city. More importantly, Atlas is the heir to the Atlas dynasty."

Dynasty? This is starting to sound like a history of European royalty. Soon she'll be telling us Atlas beheaded his wife because she couldn't bear him a strapping blond son.

"The first B.C. Atlas was an architect who designed buildings all over D.C. Then the Wagner Initiative started and forbade civs from doing certain jobs related to the arts."

"Like architecture."

"State-licensed planners began to change the look of the city, tearing down old stone and brick buildings and replacing them with concrete blocks designed to suppress creativity while promoting digestion."

"They can design for that?" Cicero clearly feels her research about art and architecture has failed her.

"Atlas bought up as much real estate as he could before it was destroyed—a few blocks, the Atlas District. He never sold it. He passed it (along with his name) down, generation after generation, preserving it."

"But weren't the buildings declared illegal?"

"Not illegal . . . Frowned upon. It seems, after doing some research . . . much of what you've been taught your whole life is a lie."

No doubt Lucy's right, but what does she really know about her own kid's life? She shoved me out the door as soon as she got the chance.

"When I was little—like five or six, I had dreams, nightmares something was chasing me. I didn't know what or who . . . I could never get away no matter how fast I ran. I'd wake up in the middle of the night, sweaty, terrified. I'd open my eyes to a big dark room full of other girls tossing and turning in their sleep. I'd run to the door and try to open it, but it was locked from the outside. I'd lay back down and close my eyes, hoping I'd wake up, but knowing all of it was part of a nightmare I couldn't escape. Don't pretend you know anything about me. Without your help, I became the best singer in my class and I plan to become the best in the world. Without anyone's help."

My mother looks like she'd been slapped in the face—pretty much the desired effect.

"I'm sorry. For everything."

Maybe she deserves a chance. This woman could have refused to meet up, stayed hidden, and gone on to live the rest of her life pretending she'd never had a troublemaking daughter. But she didn't. She's here.

"Have you met Atlas?"

"Some people say there is no Atlas anymore. That the family line died off decades ago."

"But Brax said—"

"Brax?"

"He's my . . . this guy that I was—"

"Her boyfriend." Once again, Cicero butts in with exactly the wrong thing to say.

"Ex-boyfriend. Anyway, Brax said he works for Atlas."

"Many people do. That's the way corporations work. They run on paperwork and committees. They can function forever without most employees ever meeting the person in charge or even knowing if the person in charge is actually still alive."

"So, if Atlas is dead . . ."

"Then the rebellion is dead. The state can move on to Phase II of the Wagner Initiative."

A police officer comes into the café, orders a bagel, and parks himself at a table nearby.

"I should go." Lucy crumples her napkin and stands to leave. "Brunch was wonderful. Shall we do it again next week?"

"No. I mean, I can't. I've got this . . . thing. A date." Cicero blushes and hides behind her coffee mug.

"Just us then, Darwin?" Lucy heads for the door. "See you next week."

"Wow. I can't believe it." Cicero's recovered enough to speak in complete sentences.

"I know. You have a date!"

"That's not what I was referring to."

"Newton?"

"Who else would it be? But that's what you want to talk about? Didn't you hear what she said? Rebellion? Phase II?"

"I heard. And I also saw how she shut down when Mr. Policeman came in, so shut up for now, okay?"

"What do we do now? Who can we go to for information?"

"My mother's our only source, at the moment, and I think she's done talking for right now. There's nothing we can do but wait until she's ready to tell us what else she knows."

Cicero heads in the direction of the loft. But we have unfinished business.

"Wait. We still need a place for the band to practice. You didn't think I'd forget about our new project?"

"I hoped you might, but I knew you wouldn't."

"The loft won't work. The walls are too thin. You'd hear us out in the street."

"Needs to be someplace deserted . . ."

"And soundproof . . ."

"And private . . ."

Cicero, Newton and his buddies Homer and Franklin try hard to pretend nothing strange is going on even while they cart instrument cases through the Private Library's glass doors.

Acting natural is harder than it sounds, especially when you're up to no good.

"We're actually doing this?"

Newton aimlessly flips through a MotoRama pamphlet. Beads of nervous sweat form on Homer's chubby cheeks despite the cold that follows the group in from outside. Franklin keeps his hands busy twirling his dreadlocks, and Cicero stares at the library map, though we all know exactly where we're going.

"We need one hour in the Atlas wing. I'll pay for all of us."

The same white-haired, gum-chewing librarian sits behind the desk, and she looks even grumpier this time than last time. She refuses my card.

"No need. You've been added to the wing's VIP list. You and your . . . guests . . . have unlimited access to the room, free of charge."

She leads the way down to the basement.

"Who did this? Who gave us the access?"

"Mr. Atlas." The librarian opens the door. "Stay as long as you want."

The others take a look around the room. Even though it seems secure and soundproof, we still go acoustic—no need to take unnecessary risks. Homer uses practice pads instead of a real drum set, Newton has no amp, and Franklin's keyboard is turned down low. There's a tambourine for Cicero to play, but she refuses and instead spends the whole afternoon alternately staring at the tapestries hanging on the walls and typing furiously on her tablet.

"This is the same as any other practice we've had for WI-sanctioned performances."

The singer's the de facto leader of any ensemble, and even though I've been taking charge of rehearsals for years, there's a quiver in my voice this time. Can't remember when that happened last.

"Except we could go to jail if we get caught." Franklin taps out a few chords on his keyboard.

Newton matches Franklin's chords with his guitar. "That's what makes it fun."

Cicero looks up from her tablet.

"What makes it fun is that we get to do what we love with no restrictions or stupid rules holding us back."

"So, let's get to it." Homer twirls his drumsticks.

"This is something I've been working on—Cicero and I have been working on." The lyrics from our song have already burrowed their way into my memory. "I'll start and you guys come in when you feel like it."

My eyes close and the melody flows out. No quiver in my voice. The others listen for the first few bars. Homer picks up the rhythm and taps it on his practice pads, adding the occasional fill. Franklin finds the chords and turns his keyboard to the organ setting, giving the song the eerie sound of a requiem. Newton comes in last, plucking out riffs and a solo after the second verse. By the time the song ends it's like we've been playing together for years.

"You guys . . . that sounded amazing." Cicero doesn't even try to hide the shock in her voice. She's never sat in on a music rehearsal before—this is her first experience with the rush of that very first moment when the parts come together to create a sonic whole that's bigger, better than each individual note and rhythm.

"That was like . . . landing on the moon or something." Newton stretches his fingers.

"Let's play it again."

Who is Atlas? What happened to my father? Why had the state really banned art all those decades ago? As the band plays on, the storm of questions begins to quiet. For right now, there's only this moment—a voice, a group of friends, the music, in a vacuum.

"Again."

We play the song again and again until our fingers cramp, our eyes blur and our throats go raw. Then we play it again.

Part II

When they took me, they called me Darwin Singer.
The names are the worst part.
Jokey,
stupid,
insulting.
First names are dead scientists or philosophers.
Last names are arts.
Aside from civilian clothes, old identities
are the first thing they strip away.
That makes it easier for them to control us,
to make us into who they want us to be.

8.

Maybe keeping secrets isn't such a big deal. We've all got parts of us we don't want to share. Is it ever really possible to know another person—like, know everything there is to know about them? No, we all keep secrets.

So when Brax comes back and apologizes and says that keeping secrets is a part of his job and that he wishes he could tell everything there is to tell, but he can't, it makes sense. He's just doing what we all do. Only he's getting paid for it.

It makes perfectly logical sense, which is why it's hard to explain why it hurts so much. You can't explain things that have no explanation. It's better not to even try. It's better to pretend the secrets don't exist, which is kind of the thing about secrets, isn't it? The WI trains people to become expert pretenders, actors and actresses. But it doesn't take professional instruction to know how to ignore a secret. All it takes is willpower—and of that, this girl has boatloads. Besides, there are other things to worry about.

Brax paces back and forth in his loft after giving several excuses why he can't tell me what he did on his trip and what exactly is going on between him and Atlas. His excuses go ignored.

"Who do we see about playing a show?"

"I'm sorry, what?"

"We've formed a band, and we'd like to play a concert."

"Who's formed a band?"

"My friends and I."

Brax looks like he just heard a group of Martians formed a rap group. "But you're all—"

"Geniuses?"

"I was thinking of a less flattering shared trait—you're all a part of the Wagner Initiative. Rebels don't particularly like the WI."

"All the more reason for us to do this. It's a slap in the face to the WI. And I have to be honest—none of the rebel bands I've seen so far are even remotely good."

"They're not so bad."

"They're okay for what they are—amateurs having fun. But we wanna show people what music can really sound like."

"We've got the recordings of pre-WI stuff."

"People need to hear music live—to see it up close. Feel it. So, who do we talk to about playing a show?"

At first, it's shocking to learn that the underground art movement has its own internal structure much like the state's, with hierarchy and titles and all. But it makes sense. Rebels have sprung up in pockets all over the country, all with the same interest in bringing NAA to the public, and to keep organized, the underground movements have to distribute duties among the members, electing officials, and developing policies of practice.

Each chapter's Programming Director picks which bands, dancers, poets, etc. perform at the weekly shows. This is the person National Selection (the band's name was my choice) has to impress.

Cicero, Newton, and I sit in the D.C. Programming Director's office (she—Judy—is a psychiatrist by day), three-across on her leather patient sofa, and play a recording of the few songs we've written. Judy, a middle-aged woman with blindingly white teeth, sits silent in the stiff-backed chair across from us, listening, looking as bored as if we forced her to watch cement dry. Quite the bedside manner. The intimidating doctor is worse than a room full of uptight

WI judges during end-of-the-year evaluations. Remind me never to seek this woman out if I ever need psychological help.

"What do you think?"

"What do *you* think?" Judy tents her fingers, staring each of us in the eye, one after the other.

"We think it's great." Newton has a knack for pointing out the obvious. "Or we wouldn't be here."

"Now, that's where you're wrong." Judy paces back and forth. "People come to me with a poem they've written on the back of a parking ticket they got after they've been at a hospital all day hearing how sick they are. They bring tablets filled with drawings doodled during a day of divorce proceedings. The people who come to me know that whatever they've made isn't a masterpiece . . . they don't even know what a masterpiece is, really. All they know is they want to share it, no matter how awful or embarrassing it is. It's therapy for them. And here you are, with the most technically perfect non-approved music produced since the inception of the WI."

"You really think so?" Now we can relax. Nothing like a good compliment to calm the nerves.

"I do. And that's why I have to say no."

"You're kidding."

"Afraid not. If I let you play a show, the people will riot. They've never heard music like this live, before. They'll figure out that you're WI-trained musicians and they'll be out for blood—yours. Can you handle booing and heckling and bottles being thrown at your face?"

"I don't think it'll come to that." Cicero purses her lips. "'Music hath charms to soothe the savage breast, to soften rocks, or bend a knotted oak.' Music calms people. Whenever there were riots at music events in the old days, before the WI, the violence was never because of the actual music. They were political riots, protests over ticket prices, freak accidents. The authorities looked for someone to blame, and music was the victim."

"You've done your homework. I'm impressed. People your age rarely manage to see beyond the tip of their nose." Judy stops pacing. "One night only. We'll go from there. Can you be ready by next weekend?"

We head out the door as quickly as possible, so Judy doesn't have a chance to change her mind. And so we don't change ours either.

A celebration is in order at the greasiest burger joint we can find—quite a task, since the state has recently started clamping down on what dishes restaurants are and, more importantly, *are not* allowed to serve. Pizza and burgers (the two best foods) are at the top of the hit list for their fat and sodium content. But this place, an SFL-themed brewpub with signed team jerseys, socks, and pictures affixed to every available surface, has thus far avoided the restrictions and is rewarded with a packed house.

The whole band's here, and Homer's and Franklin's girlfriends tagged along, too, all squeezed tightly into a big booth. With the noise of the crowded restaurant to drown us out, we feel safe to talk openly about the underground and the upcoming show.

"I've been playing around with costume ideas." And video ideas, and album cover ideas . . . "What about prison jumpsuits? A little nod to Dr. Croon?"

"A country music group already does that." Cicero taps her straw on her teeth and thinks. "We could all dress up like mad scientists. You know our name, National Selection? It's science . . . sort of."

"Bo-ring." Franklin's girlfriend is *extremely* helpful.

"She's right." Franklin earns a peck on the cheek. "It is boring. What about masks? I've been reading a lot of these things—comic books—and the crime fighters, the heroes, always wear masks to hide their true identities."

"Why would you want to hide your true identity if you're doing something good?"

"Because if people knew who you really were, the kind of special powers you had, you'd never get a moment's peace. Bad guys after you, trying to kill you. People like the state and scientists coming after you trying to study you and make you work for them."

"You'd never be able to go out to dinner or take a vacation, or anything. No privacy." Sounds familiar.

"Masks, huh?" Newton says. "I like it."

"Yeah," Homer says. "And people wouldn't know us right away—that we're WI."

"And if there are undercover agents, spies for the state, they won't be able to identify us." As soon as the words come out of my mouth, the whole table goes quiet.

Tonight is the first time any of us have acknowledged out loud that what we're doing qualifies as treason. We're enemies of the state, no kidding, no joking around. As soon as we step on that stage for the first time, we (or rather, the masked members of National Selection) will be criminals—wanted by a government that can make people disappear forever.

"If there are undercover agents there," Newton says, "we'll show them exactly what they've been missing."

This leads to much cheering and glass clinking, but the truth is if undercover agents are at our first performance, the presence of clearly trained musicians will send up red flags all over the place. And the presence of state agents at a super-secret, password-protected underground show would also mean that within the underground, the tight-knit group built on trust, there happens to be a traitor.

Once again my not-quite-but-almost-boyfriend has disappeared. Well, he hasn't called in days. Going between anger that he hasn't called and fear that something horrible has happened to him takes more energy than it's worth admitting.

When the latest transition from fear back to anger happens, my celly rings. Brax wants to meet up. At the White House.

It looks the same as it did to my 7-year-old self, with the sprawling lawns and the big, white buildings and statues looming over everything. Except that on that visit to the Government District, a WI field trip, the statues were terrifying to a 7-year-old who'd never seen such things before. People had turned to stone. If you were important enough, it seemed, one day they (not sure exactly who *they* were) would come up to you and say, "Okay, you've done enough. Thank you so much. Now we're turning you to stone so the world can remember you just as you are." The important people would protest, "No! I don't want to be turned to stone. I still have important work to do!" Kids are stupid like that.

The buildings, however, are as amazing now as they were all those years ago. The huge marble staircases, thick white columns, and domed roofs—relics of a time when the state was more concerned with looks, with building fancy homes for itself, than actually doing business. The Government District is, apart from the Atlas District, the only part of town where non-approved buildings are given a pass from destruction, in this case because they symbolize the infinite nature of the state's authority or some such nonsense.

And there's Brax, standing in front of the White House fence, bundled in a thick gray coat, alive and well. The anger's back.

"Where—?"

"Stop. You know I can't tell you where I've been." Brax keeps a bit of distance between him and me.

Thanks to Newton's love of fast cars and women in bikinis, old movies have been playing in our loft lately, most of them about spies—people who pretend to be one thing when they're really something else. The way Brax looks as he glances around wildly, searching for someone following him or watching him, he could be a leading man in one of those spy flicks.

"I brought you here because it's the one place they'd never expect me to. I can't see you anymore. It's not safe. I'm moving out of my loft. Don't try to find me. I won't be at the record store anymore, either. I'm sorry."

A kick in the gut. The boy with the sad eyes is the one with secrets. The boy who claims to be working for Atlas is the one who doesn't trust me enough to tell me what's really going on. This breakup should be going in the opposite direction.

He leans in to give me a hug, but there's no way that's happening. Not ever again.

"Okay, then. Darwin, I'm not a bad guy." Brax turns and disappears into the crowd of sightseers and politicians.

Standing outside the White House should stir up feelings of admiration and awe—or at least a small appreciation for how beautiful the thing is supposed to be. Instead, it's like looking into the future. One day this building too, its columns and rose gardens, will almost surely fall victim to the constant march of progress, knocked down in favor of an ugly concrete box.

The Pleasure District is quiet for a Friday night. Even on a night as cold as this one, when bars have their doors closed tight to keep out the snow, you usually see a few drunks wandering the streets, heading from one watering hole to another. But tonight the sidewalks are empty—except for me and Cicero.

"Hold it. Something's weird."

Maybe it's the two men in suits standing in front of the Private Library, trying (and failing) to look casual. Or it could be the big gray van parked at the end of the block.

Two young civs—no one we know—walk up to the library and go inside. As soon as they're through the glass doors, police officers come out from behind bookshelves and under desks and swarm, guns drawn (they brought back guns!). The two youths throw their hands in the air in terror and let themselves be handcuffed and loaded into the van waiting at the end of the street, all while trying to explain that they've never broken any laws before (okay, maybe they jaywalked once or twice) and they're only at the library to research MotoRama's new steambike. Then the van drives off, the police officers return to their hiding places—the scene resets as if nothing happened, a new gray van pulling into the old one's place.

"Let's go. I'm calling Newton." Cicero pulls out her celly as we head back the way we came.

"Tell them to meet us at our place, now."

This is it. Someone's found out. The only person who knew what we were doing was the lady inside the library, and she didn't seem to care what went on in the Atlas Wing, so long as she got her paycheck every week. But there was also Atlas—didn't the library attendant say he was the one who gave us unlimited access to the room? Doesn't that mean he knows something, too? And what about Brax? We've been sloppy. We let too many people in on the secret. We played at being outlaws as if it were a game, but now it's most definitely real.

The loft can barely hold the five members of National Selection and our equipment, but we manage. We can't manage, though, to come to an agreement on what happened at the Private Library and what we should do next.

"We told you," Cicero says. "They ambushed the two guys and threw them in a van. No questions asked."

"They must've been looking for us." The scene replays in my head. Police. Kids. Guns.

"But they grabbed people who weren't us."

"I guess they knew they were looking for someone our age doing something they shouldn't be doing at the library."

"We definitely fit that description."

"So, how did they know?"

No one can answer. Most of my theories involve Brax. Was he really protecting me? Or did he just use me for information? Does he actually work for Atlas?

"What now?"

"Let's get started. The wood floors should make us sound great."

"Practice? Here?" Cicero has the look on her face she normally saves for stepping over piles of stinking trash.

"Here's safer than the library. The store down below is closed, and the upstairs neighbor . . . he . . . moved out. We've got the whole building to ourselves."

"Let's get to it then." Franklin unpacks his keyboard.

It's clear everyone's excited to play together again, no matter the risk. Singing jingles about the benefits of a high-fiber diet isn't exactly challenging work, and playing backup guitar on tracks about proper personal hygiene can't be much better. Your mind tends to wander when you're doing work you hate, and it goes to the same places over and over again. You relive your worst moments, your worst memories replay in your head, an inescapable coda forcing you to repeat the pain of the past.

Our music pushes all that stuff away. As soon as we launch into our first song, the WI disappears. There is no Brax. There's no Atlas and no Croon. There aren't any missing fathers or absentee mothers. There's just music. Low notes, high notes, flats and sharps. If only it could stay this simple forever.

9.

The members of National Selection sit side-by-side in a metro car headed for the suburbs, instruments in cases at our feet, dressed in the craziest outfits we could each think of—Cicero, a mad scientist (she never accepted her idea was boring) in a frizzy white wig, Franklin as a comic book super-hero (we had a good laugh at the tights), Newton as someone who didn't wear a shirt and called himself Jimi Hendrix, and Homer as a caveman (why are the boys so intent on going shirtless?). I'm a wacked-out ballerina in a short purple tutu. However creative, none of our outfits are visible at the moment. Right now, we look more like a crew of bank robbers or assassins, costumes hidden under matching gray capes, upper parts of our faces hidden behind matching gray masks. The few civs in the car, their children clutched tight to their sides, probably riding back to the suburbs after a day of family fun in the city, give National Selection a wide berth.

Once we're off the train, we can relax. Hearing the band's first show would take place in the bowling alley on the edge of the city was kind of disappointing (so much for a glamorous debut). But now, walking through the deserted neighborhood streets unprotected, the lack of prying eyes feels like a blessing.

"Check this out."

Newton rifles through the cords inside his equipment case. The rest of the group gathers around him, five hooded figures huddled in the dark—we must look terrifying to someone peeking out a window of one of the cube houses.

"Here it is." Newton holds a black metal baton in his hand—like the ones the police use as part of their riot gear.

"Cool," Homer and Franklin say.

"Where did you get that?"

Newton hands the baton over. The weapon is heavier than it looks, the metal cold and jagged in spots, probably to dole out more damage. What kind of person could bring themselves to use something like this?

"Now that we're outlaws," Newton says, "I figure we need protection. Music and colorful clothes aren't the only things you can get on the black market."

"You have to get rid of it." Cicero crosses her arms. "Throw that thing in the trash right now."

"Not happening. What if someone finds it? It's got my fingerprints all over it."

Newton puts the baton back in his bag, and the band continues walking, in silence.

The bowling alley is mostly empty, like always, and the few civs there ignore the band completely as we make our way past the bouncer and through the door that leads downstairs so we can get ready for the show. Every sound we make setting up our equipment bounces off the empty basement's dingy concrete walls and echoes back at us. In the tense silence after our quick sound check, we strip off the capes and wait.

The crowd begins to trickle in. No sign of Brax.

"Looking for someone?" Cicero comes up behind me.

"Checking for new faces, potential spies."

This is the usual crew, all the familiar faces. Except for the one face in particular that won't get out of my head. With enough people finally gathered at the foot of the stage, hollering for music, the band takes our places.

"Hi." My microphone voice is a little softer and lower than normal. "We're National Selection. I hope you like us."

The first song starts quietly—a soft lyric about leaving home at a young age and feeling lost. The crowd is silent. Their expressions are blank. They're not even swaying with the beat. Our fears about everything that could go wrong during our first show are coming true. No one is getting it. These people are used to out-of-tune, off-key, nonsensical music. Maybe they don't like the group's more refined sound. Or worse, they're offended that WI musicians would dare even show up at an underground function let alone play at one. A riot could break out any minute.

No choice but to close my eyes and power through to the end of the song. Nothing. No clapping. Silence. Just when I brace for the boos and rotten tomatoes to come flying my way, there it is. A slow clap in the back of the crowd. The sweetest sound ever. The applause makes its way forward like a wave, gathering momentum, and by the time it reaches the stage, the crowd's all smiles and cheers and shouts for more. A few misty-eyed people even wipe tears from their faces.

"You like us?"

The audience noise is better than any award the WI could ever give. No one cheers like this for songs about the state. Jingles for popsoy and electrowater don't make people nod their heads and shake their hips. No one has ever cried over the tune to the alphabet song.

"You really like us?"

The crowd cheers louder. Darwin's Rule #23—Make Them Prove They Love You.

Homer taps his sticks. "Five, six, seven, eight!"

We launch into our most up-tempo song. The lyrics leap out of me and my body moves, not caring what it looks like (for once), while the crowd moves along with the music. Even Cicero's having fun, smiling and banging away on the tambourine she initially refused. This proves it. The WI has it wrong. This isn't dangerous—this music, this party, these people—it's bliss. How can something that feels this good be bad?

Out of place: two strangers in the back of the room not caught up in the frenzy, standing still, talking to each other. Their faces stand out, frowning next to all the smiles. The gray of their clothes sticks out against the rainbow-colored mob. A jolt of fear surges through my body, and I close my eyes, willing myself to just get through the rest of the song. When I open my eyes, the men in gray are gone.

The set ends. Civs pull the band off stage, desperate to shake hands and congratulate us. Program Coordinator Judy appears and gives each of us a hug.

"You're a hit. I guess you proved me wrong. Play another show next week? A bigger one? Come to my office Monday."

Civs begin to close in, shouting, tugging at our costumes and asking who we are. One civ even pulls at my mask, trying to rip it off. We pack up our gear and flee the adoring crowd up the stairs, into the safety of the bowling alley above. We don't stop until we're well beyond the parking lot, heading through the residential neighborhood toward the metro station.

"I think . . . we can stop . . . running now." Homer bends over to catch his breath.

"That was ridiculous." Newton says.

"That was nuts," Franklin says. Newton slaps him a high five.

"That was . . ."

"Cicero's at a loss for words. Enjoy it now, Newton, it'll never happen again."

Cicero sticks her tongue out. "Ladies and gentlemen. I'd like to make a toast. Please raise your imaginary glasses filled with imaginary beverages. Tonight we rocked." The small group cheers. "Tonight we are criminals. We are enemies of the state, but we're flying high above it. We're untouchable. And do you know why? Because tonight we are free."

"Here, here." We clink imaginary glasses.

Time to ruin the mood. "I saw two men in back of the crowd. They weren't smiling, or dancing, or anything. Only standing there, staring at us. Wearing gray."

"Did you recognize them? Were they the men from the library? The ones who were looking for us?"

"I don't know who they were. I do know that I want to put as much distance between myself and those men as possible. Let's move. We need to get on the train."

Only when we are safely headed back into the city and sure that no one has followed is it safe to talk. The rest of the band needs to know everything—about Atlas, Brax, and my father's disappearance.

"The state's about to pass a law banning public displays of affection." Newton apparently knows some things I don't.

"It's called 'Don't Kiss and Tell,' and it's causing riots." Homer seems to know even more than Newton. "Civs are staging mass make-out sessions all over the city."

"I had to see one to believe it." Newton smiles.

"I bet you did." Cicero doesn't look amused.

"We've heard rumors about something called Phase II."

"The conversation with Lucy—my mom—that was abruptly cut short by the appearance of a cop. She mentioned Phase II. What is it?"

"Not what, but where? Phase II is a giant prison located somewhere in the Midwest. No one knows too much about it except that the state's calling it a 'permanent solution to non-approved lifestyles.'"

"Permanent?"

"Yeah," Newton says. "As in you go there and never come back."

"Stop it," Cicero says. "You don't actually believe Phase II is real, do you? Clearly it's a rumor started to make people that much more afraid to go against the state."

"Maybe." The thought of Phase II brings up a kind of sick hope. If this horrific prison is real, my father might be there, tortured, locked away, but alive.

After the band's brief meeting with Judy on Monday (in which we agree to play a show every weekend from now until forever), it's back to work at the WI. How can a person spend their whole life working here without losing it? The gray comes at you from all sides—floor, ceiling, walls. Even your clothes are in on it. Nothing like last Saturday night and all the colors . . .

Sitting in a tiny room soundproofed with foam walls (gray foam, naturally), I rehearse a tune with another singer, a shy eleven-year-old girl, whose voice strains to hit the low notes the song about kitchen safety requires. Watching Cicero polish the baseboards would be more fun.

"We'll change the key so it'll better suit your voice."

"Yes ma'am." The girl can barely look up from her sheet music.

"Don't call me ma'am. I'm not that much older than you."

"Yes, ma'am. I'm sorry. I mean I have to call you ma'am. You've been integrated."

The girl blushes as if surprised she has the nerve to disagree with an authority figure. Maybe there's hope for this one yet.

"What's your name?"

"Tesla Carol, but people call me Tess."

"Okay Tess. I'm Darwin Singer."

"I know. Everyone knows about you."

"What do you mean? Knows what?"

"That you're famous. I mean you've won a Grammy and all."

"Oh. Right. Well, if you're a good little girl, and you do nothing but follow the rules and practice every single day, maybe you too can grow up to win an award for the best song about tooth care."

The tiny singer looks thrilled at the prospect. So much for recruiting a new rebel.

At lunch, it's time to stock up on free snacks. Whatever problems the WI has with music considered "bad for you," they have no such concern about food. Yet. That'll change once the laws do. But for now, my bag is stuffed full of snack cakes and packets of extra-salty microwave popsoy pilfered from the break room.

I pick at a snack cake while staring at the muted media screen hanging on the break room wall. The local news—always a mediocre production—shows a story about a monkey that escaped from the zoo and is now wreaking havoc in the Business District. Next, some footage of Croon's trial flashes on the screen. There are a few other people in the break room, but no one seems to care when I turn the volume up loud. The anchor describes new developments in the Croon case.

"After a record ten minutes of deliberation, a jury has found Dr. Euripides Croon not guilty of producing Non-Approved Art. We're showing Euripides Croon as he exits the courthouse."

When the anchor changes the subject, WI members begin to speculate about what happened during the closed-door trial, why Croon was found not guilty, whether he'll return to the WI, and if not, who'll take his place as lead vocal instructor. Rumor is everyone's too scared to take the job and perhaps become the next target of an investigation.

The relief at the instructor's verdict doesn't do much to get rid of the sick feeling about the whole situation. Unlike Croon, who probably never did NAA to begin with, I'm knee-deep in the underground art scene. A not-guilty verdict doesn't seem likely. While my coworkers probably have no idea what horrors lay in store for someone found guilty of NAA, I think I have a pretty good guess: Phase II. It's either a maximum-security prison where those convicted on NAA charges spend the rest of their lives locked away or a death camp—maybe some gruesome combination of both.

The long way out of the WI building leads through the dorms. Maybe the old hangout will prove to be a mood-booster, or at least bring back a good memory or two.

Reagan Twirl, Homer's girlfriend, rushes out of a dorm room and down the hallway, dressed for dance rehearsal. We don't see each other until it's too late, and the force of our collision makes Reagan drop her gym bag, the contents spilling all over the floor.

"I'm so sorry."

"Yeah right." The dancer quickly scoops up her belongings, waving my hands away when I try to help.

"Huh?" Reagan has always been kind of unfriendly, but right now she seems downright angry.

"You bumped into me on purpose. I don't have to take this. I know things."

"What are you talking about?"

"You think you can scare me? Who do you think you are?"

"I—"

"Oh, that's right." Reagan gets to her feet and slings her gym bag across her shoulder. "The great Darwin Singer. Best thing to come out of the WI since Euripides Croon. Well, look what happened to him."

Reagan runs away, down the hall, around a corner. A wave of exhaustion washes over me. The WI'll do that. It makes people tired and angry and strange. It would take too much effort to chase Reagan to try and figure out what she'd been going on about. Besides, there's no time. Four more hours training young initiates on the subtleties of instructional singing lay ahead.

Trying to teach a boy who will clearly soon be kicked out of the WI for lack of talent is a waste of time for everyone involved. What would life be like without the WI? What would I be doing? Maybe I'd be a young professional, wearing crisp gray suits and high heels, taking notes in a board meeting in a glass-walled office in the Business District. Or a server in a grease-stained apron, refilling water glasses and juggling trays stacked high with chicken fingers and onion rings. Maybe I'd have a boyfriend who played football with his buddies on the weekend instead of riding off on mysterious errands. Maybe my father wouldn't be dead and my mother wouldn't have sent me away.

The boy finishes his song. "What do you think?"

Even his speaking voice is hopelessly off-key. Now it makes sense why professors sugarcoat their criticism. This boy won't make it through another year in the WI, but telling him will crush him. I can't do it. Not today. "If you couldn't sing for the WI, what would you want to do?"

"What do you mean?"

"I mean, have you ever thought about something else you might want to be when you grow up? For pretend. A fireman . . .?"

"I guess," the boy says after some thought, "I'd want to be an astronaut. You could go explore places no one's ever gone before—do things no one's ever done. You'd be like a pioneer.

Discovering planets and treasures. What about you? What would you want to do?"

"I think I'd like to be an astronaut, too."

10.

Drinking a cup of tea in a dark corner of the café in the Atlas District is the perfect way to wallow in self-pity. So I spend a lot of time in that corner, slouched in a gray velvet armchair, with a mug of steaming chai, feeling sorry about life.

Cicero's gone on a trip to the beach with her parents, a "let's get re-acquainted" vacation. Even initiates who join the WI when they're older still spend their formative years away from home, so post-integration family relationships tend to be strained. Lucy's sick and can't make it to brunch, so the whole weekend is filled with lonely time and nothing to distract me from my thoughts, which turn darker by the minute. Croon, Brax, my father. The men in gray suits.

An old man sits alone in another gray velvet armchair in another dark corner of the café. He studies a newspaper (made of paper, not an ereader) and takes notes in a small paper pad, which wouldn't be that weird except he wears gray pajamas and matching fuzzy slippers. The gray of his hair (which matches the gray of his pajamas) reminds me of the hermits I imagined on that first trip out to the suburbs. Indeed, this man does look out of place in the city. Generally, people who live in D.C. proper are a bit hard for a variety of reasons not limited to poverty and an obsession with fitness. This man, from the wrinkles around his eyes and his plump fingers down to those fuzzy slippers, seems completely soft.

A conversation may be in order. We're the only people in the café, after all, and he looks like he hasn't had human contact in a very long time. Besides, moping around all day gets old.

The bearded old man folds his newspaper, puts his pen down, and looks over at me when I sit down next to him. He isn't smiling.

"Can't you see I'm busy?"

"I'm sorry. I thought . . . I'll go—"

"Kids." The old man frowns. "And they wonder why I never wanted any."

With that, the man looks back down at his newspaper and notes. Maybe this was a bad idea . . .

"Sit down. You're already here."

As I'm about to ask why he changed his mind, the man cuts me off. "Riots. Can you believe it? I never thought I'd see it. Not in my lifetime."

"Me neither."

"And look at this." The man turns to a story on Croon. "They've crossed the line."

"Who's crossed what line?"

"The state." The man lowers his voice. "They don't understand." He jabs Croon's mug shot with one stubby finger. "This means war."

"War with who?"

"With the state."

"Who's fighting the state?"

"You."

Clearly, the man's delusional. But he doesn't seem dangerous, so it's safe to play along.

"Me, you say?"

"And all the rest of you."

"The rest of who?"

"The underground." The man's voice is barely above a whisper.

"How do you know about the underground? Who are you?"

"Oh, I'm so sorry. I didn't introduce myself. Haven't been out of the office in a while, you see. No excuse for bad manners. None at all." He sticks out his hand for me to shake. "I'm Nobody, at your service."

"Your name is Nobody?"

"Don't be ridiculous. Does Nobody sound like a name?"

Something clicks. The chubby cheeks, the beard—this face is extremely similar to the face on the statue outside the Atlas Theatre—the statue of B. C. Atlas, himself. Well, this isn't *that* Atlas, but it's *an* Atlas. The last Atlas. The only living heir to the family dynasty. Only a moment ago, he was a gentle old man with a few screws loose. Now, he's the most wanted man in D.C.

"People think you're dead."

"Do they?" He smiles. "I did try pretty hard to convince them."

"What are you doing here?"

"Talking to you."

"You came to this café to talk to me?"

"I came for the coffee. I stayed for the conversation."

"What makes me so important?"

Atlas laughs long and hard. "Why, nothing at all, silly girl. You're not important. Don't you see? That's the beauty of it. You're perfectly average."

The Grammy on my nightstand begs to differ. What's Atlas trying to say?

"You, in most ways—all the ways that count—are like everyone else in D.C. In the world. Your clothes are wrinkled. You watch too much TV. You're never on time. You—"

"Okay, I get it. I'm average."

"In every way. That's why the movement needs you. They've got leaders and they've got fighters, but what they're severely lacking in are regular old people. They need you to show civs that you don't have to riot in the streets or stand on soapboxes making speeches. You can show them that all you have to do to make a difference is be true to yourself, at all costs."

"I'm not sure I understand."

"Take this."

Atlas reaches into his pocket and pulls out a small box printed with a picture. Nothing I've ever seen before—a drawing of a man hunched over, lifting a sphere of interconnected rings on his shoulders. The box rattles when you shake it. It's a sleeve wrapped around a tray, which holds a handful of short wooden sticks—matches, used to light fires in the old days. They've been illegal since before I was born.

"What are these for?"

"A reminder." Atlas picks up his newspaper and notebook and shuffles out the door.

My tea has long since gone cold, but holding the cup occupies my hands while my mind's busy trying to make sense of the conversation. Atlas's presence in the café was no accident. Yes, he's a nutty old man, but he's also the center of what is about to become a revolution. And he took the time to seek me out.

By the time Cicero gets home, there's another cup of tea in my hand—homemade, not nearly as good as the stuff from the café, but after the odd conversation with Atlas, something warm and comforting to hold on to seems appropriate. Sitting there, holding a now cold cup of tea, waiting on Cicero to get home so we can analyze the conversation, the situation feels especially bleak. War is coming.

Cicero flips on the lights when she comes in the door. "Why are you sitting here in the dark?"

"It wasn't dark when I sat down."

Cicero sits next to me, takes the cup of tea out of my hands and sips. "So what's wrong?"

"I met Atlas."

Cicero takes a large of a gulp of tea purses her lips. "Your tea's cold. Also: what?!"

"Atlas is alive. He's old and a little bit . . . eccentric, but . . . he says we're in for a war."

"What?"

"Stop saying 'what.' War is what! Guns and tanks and flaming arrows. Fighting and dying."

"Don't be silly. A war like that hasn't happened in a hundred years. People don't fight that way anymore."

"I'm telling you what he said. Croon's arrest is the last straw and the underground is fighting back. Atlas faked his death in order to go underground and lead the rebellion."

"And why did he tell you all this?"

"I was sitting there in the café."

"Sipping tea like you always do when you're feeling sorry for yourself?"

"Right, and this old man comes in—I didn't notice how much he looked like the statue outside the Atlas theatre at first, because of the pajamas and slippers—"

"Atlas—*the* Atlas—was wearing pajamas and slippers?"

"Will you let me finish? He comes in, sits down, and starts studying the newspaper and taking notes, like he's never seen a newspaper before or—"

"Or hasn't been out of the house in ages and is trying to catch up."

"Exactly. So I go over there and sit down and he tells me that his name is Nobody and that he doesn't want me to lead the rebellion."

"Nobody doesn't want you to lead the rebellion?"

"I know it sounds crazy . . ."

"It sounds like a double negative."

"He gave me this."

Cicero holds the matchbox up close to her face, studying the drawing of the man and the sphere on the outside. Instead of returning the matchbox, and saying something like, 'hmmm interesting,' and then going into an in-depth explanation of the drawing's mythology, the writer opens the box, pulls out a match, and strikes it on the hardwood floor. She stares at the flame as it burns down close to her fingers before she blows it out.

"Just like in the movies. Why did Atlas give them to you?"

"He said they were a reminder."

"Of what?"

"I thought you might know. The drawing on the box . . . You've been looking at a lot of art lately, right? Banned books of ancient paintings?"

Cicero snaps her fingers and searches through her ever-growing illegal ebook collection. She scans text after text until she discovers the right one.

"Not art, exactly. More like religion." Cicero looks through the book until she finds a drawing that closely resembles the one on the matchbox. "I thought this was interesting when I read it, but I didn't think much else of it at the time. Atlas isn't just a last name. Atlas is a figure in Greek mythology. He defies the gods and they punish him by forcing him to hold the cosmos, the sky, on his shoulders."

"What does that have to do with the real Atlas? Or me?"

"You said Atlas told you his name was Nobody and then said you didn't have to lead the rebellion. And you believed him?"

"Do I believe the man I talked to was Atlas? Yeah, I do. Do I believe there's gonna be a rebellion? That people really will rise up and fight the state to overthrow the government? I don't know. Do you?"

"At first I thought . . ." Cicero paces back and forth, staring at the page in the mythology book. "Assuming that there is a rebellion—and I'm not saying I think it will happen, because I don't—I thought at first that Atlas really did want you to lead his rebellion and was using some kind of reverse psychology on you. You know, telling you to sit back and watch, hoping it would make you want to do the opposite. But, then he gave you this." Cicero holds up the matchbook. "Maybe he's using this matchbox to tell you someone else is holding everything on their shoulders so you don't have to."

"But that doesn't make sense. Why would he come find me to tell me that I'm *not* special? Reverse-reverse psychology?"

"I don't know." Cicero plops down on the couch, defeated. "Judy's books don't get into that."

"You downloaded psychology books from Judy?"

"I need all the help I can get figuring Newton out."

"So, how are things?"

"We're going through a rough patch. Nothing big. It's—I hate the way he chews. We're spending too much time together, I think."

"Aren't couples supposed to want to spend time together?"

"That's what all the histories make you think, isn't it? And the NAA love stories are even worse—that Jane Eyre pining over her boss even after she finds out what a horrible guy he is. It creates unrealistic expectations."

"Speaking of relationships, I ran into Homer's girlfriend at the WI yesterday. And she wasn't too happy to see me. Would you like to shed any light on that, oh wise and knowledgeable Cicero?"

"Well . . ."

"You *do* know something."

"Homer broke up with her. She didn't take it well. She thinks you're the reason."

"Why would she think that?"

"Can't you see it? He's got a crush on you."

"Homer?" He's nice enough—not exactly the right type though. Nothing like Brax . . .

"Anyway, she thinks there's something between you two, and she's threatening to tell the authorities about the band. I don't think she will, but Newton and Franklin have been working on Homer to get him to take her back."

Something about this doesn't add up. Reagan didn't mention a word about Homer in the hallway.

"I don't think Homer's what she wants. Tell the boys to ease up on Homer. I'll handle Reagan."

"What if it really happens?"

"What if she tells?"

"No." Cicero holds up the matchbox.

"You mean what if what we're doing becomes about something more than art?"

When this whole thing started, the world was different. Before the underground, there was a girl who kept to herself, didn't have many friends, distrusted everyone. But now . . . there's a new world—one that can't exist without the people who are a part of it, new friends and old ones. A mother. Things have changed—evolved. What if it all becomes about something more than art? Easy.

"It already has."

After work, a search for Reagan in all the usual initiate hangouts—the compy lab, the game room, the cafeteria—comes up empty. My footsteps echo in the deserted hallways. The building's current abandoned state probably has something to do with the feeling of unease that's taken over the place. No one wants to be seen hanging out with anyone else, in case that person proves to be the next one arrested for NAA. Employees eat their meals alone, and initiates rehearse alone in their dorm rooms.

A faint sound comes from the practice wing. It couldn't be music because the practice rooms are soundproof. When I head that way it turns out my instinct is right. There's Reagan in a dance studio, alone, practicing an elaborate routine that seems to illustrate proper job interview etiquette. Watching the girl move for a few moments proves her skill.

The dancer turns and stumbles, startled to see someone else in the room. "What do you want?"

"I come in peace." A phrase in an NAA film about an invasion of creatures from another planet. "I want to talk."

"So, talk." Reagan towels the sweat from her face and neck.

"Not here. Let's take a walk."

We leave the headquarters and walk a few blocks.

"How would you like to join National Selection?"

My guess is jealously over the band, not the boy, is at the root of Reagan's fury.

The way Reagan raises her eyebrows tells me I'm right. "But I'm not a musician."

"National Selection isn't strictly a band."

"It's not?"

"We're more of a . . . collective, a group of like-minded people—musicians, writers—"

"And you're looking for dancers?" Reagan smiles. "Count me in. What about McKinley, Franklin's girlfriend? She's really great at posters and fliers."

"Count her in, too. Both of you come to rehearsal tomorrow night."

Reagan hurries back toward the WI. On her way to tell McKinley right now, probably.

"Reagan," I call after her, "don't tell anyone else." But the girl doesn't turn around.

11.

The night of National Selection's fifth show in as many weeks, the bouncer at the bowling alley has to turn rebels away. Most people in the capacity crowd get there early, juggling or swallowing swords to pass the time and entertain each other while they wait together for the main attraction. There've been bigger crowds, sure—the Grammys are still televised—but no other crowd can compare to this mass of rebels now working itself into an impatient frenzy.

Last week, the band got together and put our costumes to good use hanging posters for the upcoming show all over the city. Under cover of night, we went out dressed in our trench coats and masks, posting McKinley's handiwork on light poles, park benches, and public bulletin boards that were normally used for campaign fliers and lost dog notices. The posters show a mask, a date, and the location: "The Quietest Place on Earth," which all D.C. rebels know is code for the bowling alley (because it's the one place you can hear a pin drop—ha ha).

So many people show up to the show that when it's time to dive off the stage during the encore, into the crowd—they call it crowd-surfing in old videos of NAA bands—dozens of hands reach up to catch me. I'm floating along, buoyed by the crowd, passed from hand to hand, singing. My shoulders dip toward the floor, but there's no reason to doubt the crowd—when one set of hands falls away, another takes its place.

After the show, the band sits in the backstage area—a storage closet with a few folding chairs, a mini-fridge, and some old rugs thrown over crates of spare bowling balls and pins—waiting for the crowd to thin out. Judy, dressed in head-to-toe green leather (must have cost her a fortune), comes in, pulls up a chair and shares the good news.

"This is the biggest crowd we've ever had. People are here from New York to see you guys."

"Seriously?" Reagan stretches as best she can in the tight space.

"Those fliers you guys put up . . . You've brought us a lot of attention. Attention isn't necessarily a good thing. We increased security, and we've got our eyes open, but you never know who you can't trust."

A woman about Judy's age, dressed in the shortest dress and the tallest heels, pushes her way into the tiny room. She brings a frantic energy with her.

"I hope I'm not interrupting," the woman says. "Ugh, I've got to get out of these shoes. Do you mind?"

The woman leans on Newton's shoulder and uses him to prop herself up as she takes off her shoes, breathing a sigh of relief when her bare feet hit the floor. Newton blushes.

"Much better."

"Guys, this is Heloise," Judy says. "She's the New York Programming Director, the Head of Morality for the State Football League by day, and a good friend of mine when she's feeling up to it."

"I'm gonna get straight to the point because my feet hurt, and I've got a long drive ahead of me. How would you feel about moving to the Big Apple?"

"Wait a second," Judy says. "We talked about a few shows here and there."

"New York needs National Selection. We both know these kids are too talented for D.C. This place—where are we, a basement?—it can barely hold a hundred, a hundred and fifty people, tops." Heloise turns her attention to the band. "I can put you in venues that will hold a thousand people. Two thousand, even. And I'm not talking about bowling alleys. I'm talking about honest-to-goodness rock clubs. What do you say?"

"We have lives here, families." Cicero crosses her arms. *She's got family.*

"I don't expect you to move to a place sight unseen. Come up and visit first. I've arranged for you all to be invited to the big SFL conference next month—free room and board. In the mornings, attend the conference, play the new fight songs for the team owners, the high-rolling fans. . . The evenings will be yours to explore the city. And on your last night in town, you'll play your biggest show ever."

"Sounds reasonable." Homer's first words spoken in Reagan's presence since the two broke up.

"See you next month, then." Heloise and Judy head out the door.

The band sits in silence for a while, listening to the sound of tonight's volunteers sweeping the floor in the main room. Nobody else is going to ask the question.

"Who wants to move?" It's at least worth considering.

"I do." Newton says.

"Not me," says Cicero.

"Neither do I," says Reagan.

"Well, that's not a problem," says Homer. "Because we don't need you. And you either, Cicero. No offense, but Newton, Darwin, Franklin, and I are the musicians."

"Well, I want to stay," Franklin says.

"We like D.C.," McKinley says.

"Have any of you that say you want to move ever been to New York?" Cicero waits. No one answers. "I haven't either. We can't make an informed decision without visiting first, can we? I say we go to the conference, play the show, and see what the city has to offer."

From the penthouse ballroom of SFL headquarters, the New York skyline—a series of gray rectangles stretching up into the clouds—looks exactly like D.C., only bigger. Is there an Atlas District or something like it here?

"Darwin," Cicero says, as the band finishes playing Cincinnati's new fight song for about the thirtieth time in a row. "You missed the last cue."

"I'm ready to get out of here."

"Here comes Heloise." Franklin points as she makes her way towards them, a young, shaggy-haired guy in tow. "Maybe we're done for the day."

"You are." Heloise leads a few civs in a brief round of applause. "You're officially free. Go anywhere, do anything. But stay out of trouble. To help you with that—my son, Kepler." The young shaggy-haired guy waves a hand. "He'll show you around. Introduce you to some people. Say hello, Kepler."

"Hello, Kepler," he says.

"Have fun, you kids," Heloise turns on one incredibly high heel and walks away. "See you back here in the morning. Seven a.m. sharp."

"So, like, what? You want to go to the top of the State Empire building or some other touristy garbage? Cause I'm not really into that," Kepler says.

"Fine." Cicero doesn't even try to hide her contempt for his messy appearance and less-than-polite attitude. "We'll go by ourselves." Cicero heads for the elevator, the rest of the band behind her. Everyone except for me.

"Aren't you coming?"

"I'll catch up with you later."

Homer separates from the group. "Yeah, we'll catch up with you later."

"So, what do you want to do?" Kepler says.

"Show me the real New York." He seems like the kind of guy that knows where to find trouble.

"What do you mean?"

"Every place has secrets, right? Show me the part of New York the state doesn't want me to see. Show me the grimy edges."

We ride the metro with Kepler all afternoon, getting off and on at stations all over the city, touring neighborhoods and districts in all five of the boroughs. The conclusion of the outing: New York has no grimy edges. Not anymore.

"In old pictures, Chinatown is a carnival. You've seen it. Paper lanterns and dragon kites and red pagodas. What do you think?" Kepler leads us down Canal Street, between buildings labeled with signs in Chinese and English, but which otherwise look exactly like the buildings in D.C.

"Giant concrete cubes." Homer stares into the window of a bakery packed with civs waiting patiently for bread.

"And the whole city is like this? But it's twenty times the size of D.C."

So much for hoping there was a place like the Atlas District in New York. Not a single solitary brick building. Not a speck of peeling paint. The state's made sure of that. Is the Atlas District really one of a kind? What makes D.C. different? Can the rest of the country really be so completely dead?

We take the metro to Heloise's townhouse, a giant cube squeezed into a row of other giant cubes—the biggest house I've ever been inside. Kepler arms the alarm ("Mom's a little paranoid.") while Homer corners me in the entryway next to a huge potted ficus.

"So. I had fun today." Homer's standing way too close, and he reeks of musky cologne. Since when does he wear cologne?

"Me too, I guess. I wish New York wasn't so boring. I expected more."

"I could tell you were disappointed. You get this look. I don't think you even know you're doing it, but sometimes everything you're thinking shows on your face. Like right now you're embarrassed, and you want me to stop talking."

"I had no idea."

A person who plans to continue leading the double life of a WI agent by day and a rebel by night should work on controlling her facial expressions. Can Homer tell he's kind of creeping me out? Before my face can further betray me, I start walking through the house, checking out the mansion's first floor. Judging by the expensive-looking furniture, working for the SFL pays well.

"You like our house?" Kepler doesn't seem surprised. "Let me show you something you're really gonna like." He leads us toward the back of the house and down a flight of stairs.

"Let me guess. Basement." How about an attic for once?

"Huh?"

Kepler opens a door and then we're outside, looking into a garden—a mini-park, really, complete with sidewalks, groupings of trees, and a stream trickling from one end to the other, all of it blocked off from the street by the four-story houses surrounding it on all sides. Even with winter's leftover brown grass and bare trees, the garden feels alive—the dirt smell of recent planting, a slight breeze carrying dogwood petals. A man in a black hat strums a guitar on a bench, while a woman in a flowing white dress stands in front of an easel, holding a paintbrush, contemplating a tree. Young women sunbathe despite the chill in the spring air.

"You wanted secret," Kepler says. "You got it. Our private oasis, accessible only through one of the twenty-two houses lining the park. And everyone who owns one of these houses is a part of the underground. So, we have a place to come and do what we want without hiding in the dark."

The man with the guitar nods to Kepler as we stroll through the park. "He's a top-level state scientist." Kepler points to one of the sunbathers. "She's military, high-ranking."

"Seems like you know an awful lot of state people." Homer's been making vaguely hostile comments like this all day.

Kepler ignores Homer's tone. "A lot of rebels work for the state."

"Which came first? Do rebels take jobs for the state because they want to infiltrate the government? Or is working for the state so horrible that people wind up fighting the system?"

"Chicken or egg. You know the old riddle," Kepler says. "Which came first: the chicken or the egg?"

Never heard it. "What's the answer?"

"There is no answer. Or it doesn't matter. The chicken's here. The egg's here. They're both here now—it doesn't matter how they got this way. It's the same with rebels working for the state. All that matters is we're on the inside."

This trip to New York isn't a complete bust after all. The city may not impress, but Heloise's secret garden sure does. Bet that's not accidental.

"What do you do?"

"I'm a photographer," Kepler says. "I document campaigns, events—"

"No, I mean, what do you *do*? Like, outside of work. Your art."

"I'll show you."

Kepler leads us back inside and up the three flights of stairs to the top floor of the house ("Mom says elevators make you weak.") where his bedroom takes up the entire floor. Every surface is littered with pictures the photographer took of politicians and rallies outside state buildings. A large part of the room is walled off. My first thought is: closet. But only someone with a massive a sock collection would think of a room that size as storage. Plus, the door's locked. Kepler swipes a keycard and leads us inside.

The room is black for a moment before Kepler says, "Lights" and a red light blinks on. A darkroom, like the ones in old NAA films about government conspiracies—fitting, considering the circumstances.

"It's not a real darkroom. No one uses film anymore—you can't even buy it. I like the red light. It's kind of retro, right?" Kepler sits down at a compy and scrolls through hundreds of images on his computer.

"Interesting work," Homer says. "Some of your compositions seem a bit weird—"

"They're beautiful."

The photos roll by on the screen. Each picture shows a mishap—something the state wouldn't want anyone to see, let alone document. A paper cup on the sidewalk leaking brown goo, no state sanitation workers in sight. A police officer buttons up his uniform on the way to work, even though they're never supposed to be seen half-dressed. And a video. Kepler presses play. A little boy stands with his mother waiting for the metro at a crowded station. The little boy starts to hum and the mother tells him to hush. The little boy sings, loudly, and people begin to stare and move away. The mother tells the boy to be quiet, but the boy won't stop singing. Finally, the mother scoops the little boy up, covers the boy's mouth with her hand and whisks the boy out of the station.

It's almost impossible to watch. What happens to that little boy? Does his mother send him away that night, or does she teach the boy to hide his gift, so that they might spend a little more time together, holding hands at metro stations, before the state drags him off to the WI?

Kepler looks up from his compy. "Mom thinks you're special. Your band is supposed to, like, unite rebels nationwide or something. It's this big grand scheme she's got. She's always up to something."

"Your mother wants all the different groups of rebels to unite? Why?"

"No clue. But if my mom wants it to happen, believe me, she knows how to get her way."

"What makes us so special?"

"Maybe you're . . . convenient. My mom's got her own motives. Remember that. If there's something to be gained from bringing you to New York, then she plans to gain it. Hey, do you want to shoot some pictures to use as album art? I know my mom plans to record you guys while you're here. I've got a few ideas."

Kepler describes his album cover ideas, and I say "right" or "yep" whenever appropriate, but the other idea he's planted in my head already has my real attention. Heloise plans to record National Selection and use the band (and those recordings) to unite rebels nationwide. Heloise plans to build an army. And if histories have taught me anything about the way the world works, it's that armies are good for one thing and one thing only. War.

12.

Homer's squished against me, the two of us smushed inside a metro car crammed full of rush-hour commuters. The drummer's rank cologne creeps up inside my nose. A sneeze threatens to come out.

"Are you okay?" Homer can't really see my face from the angle he's standing at.

"I'm fine. It's just . . ." It needs to be said, and there's no time like the present. "Are you wearing cologne?"

"Do you like it?"

"I think maybe you went a little overboard. It's making me sneeze."

"Sorry. It's new. I wasn't really sure how much to use."

"Why are you wearing it?"

The train stops, and a few commuters get off, giving us a little more room—enough to put a few inches between us.

Homer grabs hold of a support bar to steady himself. "I dunno. I thought some people liked cologne."

"What about you and Reagan? I heard you guys might get back together?" That's a lie, but this line of questioning seems the best way to figure out if Homer really does have a crush on me.

"Where did you hear that? No chance. That girl is too high-maintenance. It was always, 'take me here, buy me that, rub my feet.' What about you and Brax? Can you trust him?"

The relationship with Brax is most definitely not based on trust. But what is it that blocks thoughts of anybody else? Brax is charming, but Homer is sweet—if annoying at times—and *he'd* never walk out, that's for sure. Brax is absolutely better looking, but who's shallow enough to keep drooling over a hot guy even after he dumped you?

"So you guys are over? Because you deserve better."

He's right. But, you grow up denying every urge you have in favor of following regulations. When you finally get that first taste of freedom, you're like a horse running wild, jumping fences, following every instinct even when it leads to trouble. You realize the danger, but you're just not sure you can rein yourself in . . . even though you know it's best to give up the Braxes of the world in favor of the Homers.

The band meets up at a restaurant in New York's Pleasure District—an Indian place on the bottom floor of the New York City jail. The jail is about five times as big as D.C.'s and takes up around three city blocks. Its bottom floor, with glass walls, seems to be prime real estate, home to expensive stores and fancy restaurants where you go if you want to be seen. The band chose the least fancy restaurant located beneath the jail, this Indian place, fittingly enough called Sitar.

"Heloise wants us to record an album." We're swapping accounts of the afternoon with the rest of the crew (leaving off the part where Homer follows me around like a puppy). "And she wants to send it out to rebels all over the country."

"I didn't know there were rebels all over the country," Franklin says.

"We're gonna be famous." Newton smiles through a mouth full of curry.

"Infamous, more like it." Cicero folds the napkin in her lap over and over again. "I was fine with writing a couple songs, playing a show in a basement now and then. But this? It's becoming too much."

"You're right. We're not kidding around anymore." It's time we got serious. "I think this is about to become something more than any of us had thought. I want to ask you—all of you: Are you in or are you out? Every one of us knows the risks—jail . . . worse. I believe in what we're doing, and I plan to see it through to the end—whatever that may be. So, who's with me?"

The table falls silent. The others seem to be thinking. How can they not be absolutely sure this is the right thing to do?

"I don't think I can do it," Cicero says. "I . . . Darwin, do you know what you're asking?"

The goal's become clear: destroy the WI. We all seemed to want the same thing in the beginning, but now . . . Maybe this has become a one-person journey.

"I'm out, too," McKinley says.

"You've barely been in," Homer says. "I'll do it. I'm with you."

"No," says Reagan. "I'll do this one last show with you guys, but that's it."

"I can't do it," says Franklin. "I'm sorry."

"But—" Homer says.

Begging won't help. "Newton? We need you."

"I know." Newton looks from me back to Cicero, who stares down at her hands.

"Don't make your decision for my benefit," Cicero says. "It's your life."

Newton takes a deep breath and exhales slowly. He puts his hand over Cicero's.

"I'm sorry. I have to do this. Music is my life. You have no idea."

"I think I might. Listen, you guys don't need me in the band. You can write your own songs. I have my own writing I need to do—a novel I haven't had time to finish. I'm not abandoning the cause."

"No one said you were." It's time to make a toast. "To those of you sticking around, thank you. To those of you taking another path, good luck. I hope one day we can play together again, without fear."

While the rest of the crew spends the next few days touring the city, the members of now-shrunken version of National Selection become near-permanent fixtures in the recording studio at SFL headquarters, reworking songs to compensate for Franklin's absence, writing new material, and finally recording our music, creating concrete proof of this foray into illegal art. It was always leading to this, wasn't it?

The recording studio's nestled in the corner of a floor of SFL headquarters that also houses the building's broadcast and photography studios. It, like all the other studios, is accessible only by reciting a code into a microphone outside the door. Unlike all the other studios, the recording studio is soundproof (not only good for making high-quality recordings of fight songs, but also for making illicit rock records). Heloise changed the access code and "forgot" to distribute it to the rest of her team. She knows how to work the system.

"Why are you doing all this for us?"

I sip a cup of hot tea with honey sitting in the sound booth with Heloise. Through a pane of glass, we watch Newton record the last few of his guitar tracks, swaying back and forth to Homer's beat as it plays in his earphones, surrounded by gray foam ceiling and walls. My throat's raw (that's what the tea is for), and tonight's show will be rough, but there's Darwin's Rule #3—The Show Must Go On. For now though, New York's Programming Director needs to cough up some answers.

"I'll be honest with you." Heloise sips her own cup of tea. "I'm doing this for the money. Not for myself. As you know, I'm doing quite well, financially. But what we need to do is get certain people, influential people, to believe that art—music in this case—isn't the enemy. We need to show that art is beneficial to society. And the simplest way to do that is to show that art has the ability to make money."

"We're selling the recordings? I thought we'd give them out at shows." Should have seen this coming. Something felt off about the woman from the start—turns out she really is a greedy capitalist who doesn't care about anything but money. Instinct: 1, Trust: 0.

"I'm thinking we can move easily a thousand or two copies tonight at the show."

"And where will the money go?"

"Into a fund."

"What kind of fund?"

"Listen, don't worry so much about the details. Sing your little heart out and everything will be fine."

"I may be sixteen years old, but I'm not a child, and I'd prefer if you didn't treat me like one. Tell me what you plan to do with our money or we walk."

Heloise smiles. "You've got guts. You'll need them. The money is going into a fund that'll be used to pay for your national tour. I didn't want to bring it up yet. I was hoping to wait until after tonight's show when you saw how huge this could be."

"And you want us to tour so we can unite rebels nationwide?"

"Yes. But not only you. I've recruited acts from all over the country. While you're in Chicago, a dance troupe from Seattle might be in D.C., and actors from Atlanta could be heading to New York. All of them WI-trained."

"So, once all the rebels have rallied around these über-talented acts, what then? We march on D.C.? Protest in front of WI headquarters? Stock up on bayonets and storm the White House?"

Heloise sighs. "Atlas found you? He's got this idea in his head about a war. It's all these old movies he watches alone in his office. He lives there, you know. I keep telling him things don't work that way any more. You can't grab a few hundred people and a few hundred guns and take over a country. It's impossible."

Heat rises up my neck into my face—my embarrassment's showing, no doubt. How silly to believe in Atlas and his rebellion. Now, it sounds like that first impression of the man in the café wearing his pajamas and slippers was right all along. Atlas is a foolish old man who believes in fairy tales.

"It's not how things are done," Heloise continues. "You go through the proper channels, work the system. But first, we have to sell some albums. And if we plan to do that, your voice has to be working tonight. Go back to the hotel and get some rest."

"What do you know about my father?"

"He fell off a ship during a routine dedication ceremony."

"How do you—?"

"I read your file. I read up on all of you. Looked into your psych evaluations. I had to find out what I'd be dealing with—make sure you and your friends could handle the pressure. The last thing we need is another unstable personality tampering with things."

"And what did my file say?"

"That you're an intelligent young woman who is used to doing things on her own. You have a healthy sense of self-confidence that can sometimes become arrogance. Your independent streak leads you to isolate yourself from others. You're prone to breaking rules for the sake of breaking them, and you have a massive, illegal sock collection. In other words: mostly harmless."

"They know about the socks?"

It's funny. It should be infuriating that the WI analyzed my personality without me knowing, but the person that file described isn't me—not anymore. Isolated? No way—there's Cicero and the band and the rebels. Arrogant? Well, maybe. But this thing with NAA has gone too far to be some childish way of acting out. Harmless? Thinking that sock collection was a secret all these years . . . the WI has been looking the other way on purpose. They gave me a small bit of freedom in order to keep me under control. Clever. Was the state doing the same to everyone? Letting civilians get away with pulling their socks up over their pants, so they wouldn't notice all their other freedoms (to sing, to dance, to kiss in public) being slowly, systematically taken away?

"Now you see what we're up against."

The first thing to do back in D.C.: Find a way to sneak a look at my father's file. There's a chance reading his file could give some clue about his death, or reveal a way to fight back against the WI.

A nap and a cup of coffee later, it's time to head down to the hotel lobby to meet Cicero. The lobby's a large open space, sparsely decorated with hard, uncomfortable plastic furniture (clearly, they don't want anyone hanging around down here). Civs wander in and out. This meeting seems like the first time we've been alone together in ages. Lately there's always been someone else around—usually Newton with Homer in tow.

"It's time for some serious girl talk," Cicero says. "Tell me what you found out from Heloise."

One reason to love my roommate: When anyone else might want to talk about guys, Cicero wants the scoop on our latest scheme.

"I didn't find out much. She plans to sell the music and send us on a national tour."

"Newton told me. Sounds like she wants to bring some politicians over to our side."

"What makes you say that?"

"You can't really believe all that money will go to plane tickets and hotel rooms. Plenty'll be left over, and I bet she intends to spend it in D.C., buying favors from politicians."

"But bribery is—"

"Illegal? Yes, but lobbying isn't. She throws some gifts and fancy dinners at a few politicians, they write up a petition to examine the effects of WI on society, paid for by the rebels' fund. That study will show that art isn't harmful and is in fact beneficial. Congress will vote to repeal the Wagner Initiative."

"It's that simple? Then, we've won."

"Nothing is ever that simple. Not even politics."

"Atlas is a misguided old man. Heloise told me. A fight's not happening. We'll have to hope her plan to win over some politicians works."

"And if it doesn't?

"Things will stay the same."

"We've come too far. Things will never be the same."

"I know." Even if NAA never becomes legal, we've come too far to stop trying. "I asked my mother pull my father's file."

"Why would the state kill your father? That's what you're thinking, right? That they killed him or shipped him off to Phase II? It doesn't make sense. If what Heloise told you about Atlas is true—that there is no revolution, then the state would have no reason to kill your father. The government may be a lot of things, but it's not pure evil."

What's happening here? Isn't Cicero on board? Sure, she quit the band, but she's working on her own illegal art, a novel.

"Of course you're defending the state. Sweet little Cicero Wordsmith, who never broke a rule in her life—until she met me. The dress code, the art ban, the children taken away from their parents in the middle of the night, and you're saying the state's not evil? Then who is? Who's the villain here?"

Cicero sighs. "Maybe there isn't one."

The words to argue with her just don't come. Cicero's right. It doesn't make sense for the government to have killed my father. But when you've spent your whole life resenting the state, it's hard to feel any other way. All the WI has taught me, all the friends I've made, the fact that I never had to worry about food or clothes or whether I'd have a job when I grew up . . . none of it's worth what they took from me.

Maybe it's not the WI, though. The person who gave the order to take me from home was just following orders herself. And her boss was following orders dictated by a law passed decades before he was born. So who's really to blame? No one. Everyone.

"Chicken or egg."

"What?"

"It doesn't matter how things got the way they are or who's to blame. It only matters what happens from here on out."

"We have to change things."

"We will."

We sit for a while longer, watching civs come and go in their gray suits and dresses. They aren't helpless captives of an evil tyrant. They're willing participants. Maybe one of these men started the petition to ban public displays of affection. Maybe one of these women will vote yes to ban kissing in public when it comes time to cast her ballot on "Proposition Prude," as rebels call it. Maybe that purse-lipped old woman with the walker really is offended when she sees people making out on the street and will breathe a sigh of relief knowing she'll live out the rest of her life free from such lewd displays. If all of these people can be happy about things the way they are, why can't I?

13.

Tonight's the last night of the SFL convention, and a game between New York and Detroit is set to inaugurate New York's brand new stadium, Central Park Dome, a gleaming mass of glass (so non-ticketholders can see all the fun they're missing), built smack in the middle of the park. Thousands of civs wearing their team's colors and chanting their team's songs take their seats, unaware that below them, hundreds of rebels flood the maze of maintenance hallways in the bowels of stadium, where National Selection prepares for our biggest show yet.

We set up our equipment in Central Park Dome's basement, a cavernous space easily 10 times the size of the bowling alley in D.C., destined to house pre-game and halftime-show props once the stadium has built up a collection. Even though the game hasn't started yet, the muffled roar of the crowd above echoes down here, making it sound like we're in the belly of one of those dragons Cicero's been reading so much about lately.

Concertgoers come in little by little, but by the time the game kicks off, the basement's nearly full. Heloise puts Cicero in charge of selling recordings and t-shirts and prints of McKinley's posters, which are perfectly drawn portraits of me, Newton, and Homer that she made without our knowing. Cicero raises a fist in the air with each hundred demerits she makes. By the time the band starts into our opening number, our newly inaugurated merchandising specialist has already sold three thousand demerits worth of National Selection gear.

We play for over an hour, but I could stay on stage forever. Applause never gets old, and tonight's crowd is large and generous with praise.

"Thank you for coming." Heloise signals for us to wrap the show. "We're National Selection, from D.C. Let's slow it down a bit."

The crowd boos. We launch into our last song, my favorite, the one that brought tears to the crowd's eyes the first time we played it in D.C. Not quite the same reaction here in New York. Some people throw their hands up in disgust. Some people walk out.

"Play something faster," someone yells.

Angry faces stare up at the stage. Instead of stopping the song (Darwin's Rule #17—Never Give in to the Crowd's Demands), I reach up and pull back the mask covering my nose and eyes. At least some of the civs have to know my face—the child Grammy winner. What will they think now? I keep singing, my true identity exposed, staring into the faces of anyone in the crowd who'll meet my gaze. The booing and heckling fade. The song ends. Silence. And then, wild applause.

"Thank you. I'm Darwin Singer and—"

Newton grabs a microphone. "I'm Newton Stringer!" He rips off his own mask.

"And I'm Homer Thump." Homer pulls the mask from his face, too.

We leave the stage to shouts for an encore, but there's nothing left to give. My throat's raw—no voice in the morning, probably. This whole trip to New York has been painful, but worth it. Time to head backstage to decompress.

No sooner has the door shut than it bursts back open. Brax. He looks different—he's cut his hair and lost some weight, but it's Brax.

"You're in danger," Brax says. "You have to stop everything you're doing. The band, everything. You don't know what you're getting yourself into."

"Well, good to see you, too."

"This isn't a game."

"You think I don't know that? I watched my professor get hauled off to jail. They made my father disappear."

"Who made your father disappear?"

"The WI. The state. I don't know."

"That's the problem. You don't know what's really going on."

"And you do? So why don't you tell me instead of making mysterious proclamations?"

"The WI isn't part of the state. It's a private organization started as an effort to sanitize music and films—a group of conservative people trying to get rid of sexual lyrics and violence on TV. Simple as that. The group expanded to include a company that produced so-called clean art that was educational, patriotic, and moral. It was also boring. No one bought the recordings or watched the films, so the WI found a way to force them to. It raised money, lobbied for strict government regulations on art, and won. The tiniest violations led to huge fines, making it so expensive to produce art that independent artists couldn't survive. Eventually, the large production companies and record labels went bankrupt, too. The WI became the only game in town, and they got rich. People would rather listen to boring music than no music at all."

"Why did you come here?"

"To warn you."

"You dumped me, remember? Now all of a sudden you care?"

"They have the money and power to do anything to stay on top. That's what makes them dangerous. And we all work for them."

"We? I thought you worked for Atlas."

"The WI hired me to spy on Atlas, and Atlas pays me for information about the WI."

"So, the WI knew you were spying on them and happened to let slip this huge piece of information that could ruin them?"

"No. Atlas told me."

"You're as crazy as he is. There's no conspiracy—no war. You've let yourself get caught up in Atlas's delusions. Where's his proof?"

"I don't know."

"Then how can you believe him?"

"He's my father."

Of course. The same chubby cheeks. The same wide mouth.

"You're the last Atlas?"

"Braxton C. Atlas, the ninth. My father sent me to infiltrate the WI. He wanted them to think the family had changed our ways—that we were finally coming around to their way of seeing things. He actually had me walk in the front door and apply for a job. I should've known then that his mind was starting to go. They did offer me a job: to spy on my father, to tell them how he spends his days sitting around watching movies in his pajamas. The WI won't even let me in the building. I send my reports via email. The information I give my father is whatever you'd read in the paper—the WI's latest campaign against belly fat or non-orthopedic shoes. He thinks it's valuable intel."

"Do you really believe all that stuff your father told you? About the WI being a giant, greedy company?"

"Yes. No. I don't know. I wish I did. If I could prove, once and for all that my father's theories aren't true, he might give up this whole revolution idea and accept that the WI isn't trying to harm us, that maybe they're trying to help. He wasn't always this way, you know—a crazy pajama man. He used to be a real activist, filing lawsuits and starting petitions."

Newton and Homer burst into the dressing room, laughing and nudging each other, discussing some groupies they met. The laughter stops when they spot Brax.

"Meet me at Atlas Real Estate when you get back to D.C." Brax walks out the door.

The boys stare at me staring at the spot where Brax has just been, my heart beating so hard you could almost hum along with the rhythm. Brax—Braxton C. Atlas, the ninth—has just warned me things aren't as they seem, and that there's serious danger, and all I can do is be thrilled he cares? It's pretty disgusting.

Between hiding in the loft and standing in the alley behind Atlas Real Estate waiting for Brax or someone to answer the door, the next few days drag on. Some vacation days off work, a canceled National Selection show, and plans to pass the hours at home writing music become a week of staring at the media screen all day. Thankfully the band's faces never show up on the news as "Most Wanted." Once stories about the upcoming elections and Proposition Prude get old, dozens of NAA films provide a needed distraction. There's one about an altogether unremarkable, ordinary-looking girl who falls in love with a handsome, charming vampire, and somehow that blood-sucker reminds me of Brax.

Better call my mother. Even though we're talking more, our conversations still feel like awkward chatter with an acquaintance rather than real talk between family. But advice is needed and mothers are the traditional source for that kind of wisdom.

We meet in the Business District at the Approved Art Museum, built where the American Art Museum stood until only a few years ago, when the WI really started pushing for the destruction of buildings that didn't meet its standards for design (bland, plain, and bland). The old, crumbling building had marble staircases and huge white columns. Or were the columns brick?

My mother and I walk through the new lobby, a small space filled with life-sized animatronic figures made to look like famous WI members of the past that greet you as you walk into the museum. Dressed in the outdated fashion of their various decades (speedsuits, cardigans), the not-quite-human-looking robots introduce themselves one by one, and each plays a brief tune on its instrument of choice. Then they join together in playing the national anthem, and you're trapped in the room until the uncanny figures finish their off-key tune, at which point the door that leads into the rest of the museum swings open.

We wander through the empty museum, greeted at every turn not by pastoral landscape paintings or provocative nudes, but by artfully drawn depictions of the voting process and sculptures of politicians kissing babies. At first, we talk quietly about the weather and Lucy's job, but now a silence falls, only our footsteps echoing through the empty halls. Time to start asking the real questions.

We step into a listening room, choose a song about landscaping regulations, and turn the volume up loud. If someone's eavesdropping, hopefully they'll only hear two women muttering beneath a man singing the virtues of neatly trimmed hedges.

"How much do you know about the WI?"

"What do you want to know?" Lucy paces in the small room.

"Do you know that it's a private organization?"

"Who have you been talking to? It doesn't matter that the WI is private. It's got serious influence with the state."

"But doesn't that mean that NAA isn't actually illegal? It's like you said about the architecture in the Atlas District. It's only frowned upon? If it's not illegal, then how did they arrest Croon?"

"Who knows? I'm sure they thought of something. They can arrest you for crossing the street the wrong way these days. He probably admitted to not following regulations, and they made him pay a huge fine and then forced him to sign a confidentiality agreement to keep quiet about the whole thing."

"So the WI is just a powerful corporation."

"The key word there is powerful. I'm pretty sure the WI got rid of your father because he planned to start a public outcry. That card I gave you, with Atlas's initials on it—that card belonged to your father. He was working with Atlas."

The song ends, and a man walks by the closed glass door and glances inside. There was no one anywhere else in the gigantic museum. Odd that another patron would show up now, here. Another song starts up.

"I have to find out what happened to my father, and I have to finish what he started."

"I know we're not best friends, and maybe I haven't been a very good mother. I should have found you sooner. No reason for me to stay away except—"

"The WI threatened you?"

"I came to visit you some, in the beginning. You were so young you don't remember . . . but every time I looked at you it reminded me of him. And every time I had to leave, you'd cry. It was too much. I thought if I stayed away, it would be better. For both of us."

The man in the hallway has moved on. Maybe he's already heard everything he needed. Maybe what he heard didn't satisfy him. Hearing my mother confess that it wasn't threat of violence that kept her away made her seem more . . . real. For so long, she was a dark figure in my imagination, a monster who tossed her daughter aside. Now she just seems like a frightened, sad widow.

"What I'm trying to say is don't do it. Don't go chasing after your father."

"Why not?"

"Because you might find him. Whatever happened to him could happen to you, too. The WI made your father disappear. You don't think it could do the same to you? You're not afraid? What makes you so special?"

"Nothing. I'm not remarkable in any way, as people keep pointing out."

My mother can't say anything more before I'm out of the listening room, and the animatronic WI band barely has time to begin its farewell song before I'm on the street, heading back toward the metro station. What right does Lucy have to tell me what to do? None.

She's right, though. Something bad could happen, something unthinkable. But, after everything—the smiling, dancing rebels of D.C. and New York, the corruption—the unthinkable has become a tolerable risk. For me, anyway.

"Maybe that makes me special." No one's around to hear.

The sound of Cicero's celly ringing and then a one-sided conversation that's mostly Cicero saying "no" and "what?" and "oh no" is a harsh way to wake up. Cicero rushes into my room, still wearing her pajamas, not even bothering to pretend to knock on one of the makeshift walls.

"Newton called."

"Do you realize what time it is?"

"The state raided a rebel show last night. Franklin's in jail."

"What?"

"You were supposed to play that show, weren't you? But you cancelled?"

"What was Franklin doing there?"

"He got passed over for an American Society of Clean Music award. I guess he was out letting off some steam. What I don't understand is how they knew the time and location of the show."

"Brax."

"Excuse me?"

"It must've been Brax. He works for the WI."

"I thought you said he worked for Atlas."

"He does."

"But—"

"Listen." I throw on some clothes from the dirty pile nearby, and drag Cicero toward the door. "Franklin will be fine."

"Where are we going? I'm not dressed."

"You're dressed enough."

The cafe downstairs has just opened for the day, empty inside except for the barista. Not who I was hoping for.

"Have you seen an old man, plump, probably wearing pajamas and slippers?"

"Yesterday, actually," the barista says. "He left this for you." He hands me a napkin covered in scrawled handwriting. "To: the girl with curly hair" and a phone number. The rest is illegible.

Thankfully, the number works. A familiar voice answers.

"Mr. Atlas? This is Darwin Singer. I have a friend who needs your help."

14.

Cicero and Newton are about to see the big un-marked building in the Business District that started it all. But today, we won't head down to discover old pop music in Atlas Real Estate's basement with Atlas's teenage son. Today we're here to see the man himself.

We go down the alley next to the building and walk up to the back door. Unlocked. Inside is the landing that leads either down into Irregular Records or up into the rest of Atlas Realty. The door that leads down is locked. So we head up, through a heavy iron door, and are immediately greeted by a security guard and a metal detector, as well as a receptionist who seems well prepared to turn the three of us away until she discovers the appointment in her compy. She leads the way through the massive lobby, with its polished concrete walls, floors, and benches hard enough to fit right in with the décor at the WI, where comfortable seating is just another sin to ban. The receptionist guides us into an elevator, swipes a keycard and then presses a button labeled P.

"He's expecting you," she says, stepping out of the elevator and letting the doors shut behind her.

We ride up to the top floor in silence. No doubt we'll soon be confronted with the little old man from the café, changed out of his slippers, the haze of confusion gone, now sitting behind a desk waiting to give answers to every question we have. But when the elevator doors open, we stand facing a haggard Atlas, still in his pajamas, pacing back and forth, muttering to himself, in a room that was clearly once an office, but is now his primary living space, the desk pushed aside to accommodate a big, cushy sofa loaded down with blankets and pillows. Stacks of newspapers are piled waist-high, and a media screen blares a reporter's account of the raid from last night.

"Mr. Atlas?"

"Hmm?" He seems to come out of his stupor, righting his pajamas and attempting to make up the couch that serves as his bed. "Who are you?"

"I talked to you on the phone. Remember?"

A flash of recognition crosses Atlas's face. "You're the unimportant girl I met in the café. Who are your friends?"

"I'm Cicero Wordsmith."

"And I'm Newton Stringer."

Atlas gives a little nod. "Of course. So nice to meet you. I've read your work, Miss Wordsmith, and I've listened to yours, Mr. Stringer. Best the WI has ever seen."

"Thank you," the couple says in unison.

"Of course, compared to real music and literature, the WI-sanctioned drivel you two produce is quite mediocre."

Cicero purses her lips. "Now wait a second—"

"Well, now that the introductions are out of the way," I say, "we'd like to talk about our friend, Franklin—the one who's been arrested."

"It's a good thing you came to me."

"So, you'll pay his fine?"

"No." Atlas goes back to pacing back and forth in front of the media screen and muttering to himself.

"Darwin, I thought you said he would help us," Cicero says. "He's no hero; he's a doddering old curmudgeon!"

"Why won't you pay the fine?"

"I can't."

"What do you mean?" Newton says. "You're loaded."

"It's not that, young man. They've gone and changed the game. They found out about me—about the revolution. But how?"

"I think I may have an idea." It all comes back to Brax. "You hired your son to spy on the WI for you."

"Yes, maybe they followed him back to me."

"No, they hired him to spy on you."

The real estate tycoon plops down on one of the couches. "Brax? No, no, no. He's my son. He's my . . . He's everything to me."

"I guess you were just a paycheck to him," Newton says.

"How do you know all of this?"

"Brax told me himself. I'm sorry."

"Wait." Atlas perks up a bit. "If he told you this willingly, that must mean he's still on our side."

"I don't think he's on anyone's side but his own."

"Thank you for telling me," Atlas says. "But I still can't help your friend. The WI ramped up its efforts to make NAA officially illegal once and for all. It's pushed a bill through Congress, and while they're waiting on the vote, everything related to NAA is in a holding pattern, including prisoners. No more fines and easy outs. Nothing I can do except pay for a lawyer, which I will."

"That's it?" Newton says.

"Listen, kids, I'm not sure who or what exactly you think I am . . . I've been locked in this room for years trying to continue the work of the original Braxton C. Atlas, fighting the good fight. But the more I do, the less it seems to matter. After all this, I'm just a man who happens to find himself in a family with a famous name."

"How can you say that?" Cicero says. "Hundreds of people are locked away in jail, counting on you."

"I'll do what I can, but I think maybe the rebellion is a lost cause."

"A woman in New York's working to unite rebels all over the country."

"Unite rebels? I didn't know."

"That's because you keep yourself locked in here like a hermit," Newton says.

"Will you help us?"

Atlas looks back at the media screen. The footage from last night runs in a loop, a montage of police launching smoke bombs and using tasers on fleeing civs, who collapse to the ground, stunned.

"What can I do?" Hard to tell if Atlas is asking us or himself.

"For starters," Newton says, "put on some pants."

"And then we're taking a trip to New York."

Atlas may not be the best judge of character. He had no idea about his own son's involvement with the state—but putting him face to face with Heloise will surely reveal . . . well, something.

With a clean-shaven, neatly dressed Atlas in tow, we head for the nearest metro station. Once inside, we struggle to push past a large crowd gathered near the turnstiles. Civs jostle for position near the front of the crowd, where something on the wall has caught everyone's attention.

Newton pushes his way into the middle of the crowd, rips a piece of paper off the wall, and pushes his way out again. He holds it up—a poster featuring the cover photo from National Selection's album—the group in trench coats and masks, with the phrase, "Have you seen these criminals?" emblazoned across the bottom.

"They're offering a reward. Ten thousand demerits for each band member found." Newton crumples the poster and tosses it in the trash. "Dozens more of these on the wall."

An excited civ pushes his way out of the crowd. "That could feed us for months." In his hurry, he bumps into me. "I'm sorry, miss."

"No worries." Thankfully he doesn't recognize any of us.

More posters hang on the tile walls on the train platform, bigger posters, black and white ones, full-color ones. They scroll across media screens overhead. A few moments of pretending they're advertisements instead of wanted posters eases the anxiety, but that fantasy proves hard to keep up when I sit down on the train next to a composite sketch of what I might look like without the mask. The face looks nothing like mine, thankfully, but they got one thing right—my mass of unruly curls. Maybe it's time to start wearing hats.

Newton admires his composite. The Newton in the sketch looks fierce, with a chiseled jaw and piercing eyes—again, nothing like the real Newton.

"Pretty spot-on, I'd say."

"You wish."

Cicero ponders her own sketch—the artist wrongly guessed her to be brunette underneath the clown wig. And to be a guy.

"At least they're all pretty awful. No worry there."

"I'd worry about the reward they're offering," says Atlas. "That kind of money will turn friends into enemies pretty quickly. Do you know anyone who could turn you in?"

"What about Reagan?" The girl always did seem a bit self-centered, but could she be selfish enough to trade her friends for money? "Before I asked her to join National Selection, she said she knew things. It sounded like a threat."

"Reagan talks a lot, but she's harmless," Cicero says. "What do you think, Mr. Atlas? Someone you trusted turned on you."

Atlas looks at the wanted poster for a while before answering. "I don't think we can rule out the possibility that one of your bandmates would offer you up in exchange for their own freedom."

"We're doomed. No one can help us." A headache's coming on. Rubbing my forehead doesn't help, but it's the only thing in my power to do right now.

"Darwin Singer," Cicero says. "I've never known you to give up. And I've also never known you to need anyone's help. You've come this far on your own, haven't you?"

"We've had help, but everyone who's helped us also managed to help themselves. Brax gathered information for the state.

Heloise wants money or power. And you, Atlas, I think you want all of this to end, one way or the other, so you can be left alone."

"I won't deny I'd like to live my life as my own man, not having to live up to the Atlas name."

"Everyone's out for themselves." As nice as it would be to believe in the generosity of other people, the world has proven to be filled with one selfish person after.

"What about Lucy? Your mother helped us. And she didn't want anything in return. Sometimes people do things because they're the right thing to do."

We ride in silence until New York. The train begins to slow. A teenager in a gray hooded sweatshirt, the only other person in the metro car, stands up and pulls the emergency stop. As the alarm sounds, she approaches the group and stands in front of us, her hands in her pockets.

"I think I can help." The girl pulls back her hood to reveal pale skin and stick-straight dyed-gray hair. "I'm Edison Caster, but you can call me Edie. We have to get off this train."

As the train skids to a stop, Edie pries at the doors with her fingers while the rest of us look on in stunned silence.

"Are you gonna sit there staring all night or will someone help me get these doors open?"

Atlas is first to react. He goes to Edie's aid, but doesn't appear to lend much strength, as the doors still won't budge. Newton and Cicero join in the effort, to no avail. I join in and after some minutes of pulling, the five of us manage to pry the doors open. We look out into a dark tunnel. The strange newcomer steps off the train and drops out of sight.

"Come on."

Edie walks in an access path next to the train. Might as well jump down, too. The rest of the crew follows, with Atlas bringing up the rear, Newton helping him step down as gently as he can.

"Follow me. We've got to get as far away from this train as possible."

We walk along the narrow ledge next to the train, passing door after door that probably leads to the surface. Edie tries each door, and finds each one locked.

"Why do we need to get away from the train?"

"Are you blind?" Edie tosses one of the "wanted" posters at me. "Your faces are plastered all over the place."

"Those posters don't look anything like us."

"Oh really? Then how did I know they were you?"

"She's got a point," Newton says.

"So, you recognized us from the posters. Then, you must also know that the three of us are worth thirty thousand demerits. How do we know you're not leading us right to the police to claim your reward?"

Edie tries another door and the handle turns. She opens it. Inside is a stairway leading up.

"You'll have to trust me."

Edie walks through the door and holds it open. Odds and human nature say that Edie will turn us in—only a fool would walk right into this trap.

"Darwin?" Cicero says. "Are we going through?"

It's possible (but unlikely) that this strange girl isn't an enemy. That possibility (despite the score being Instinct: 1, Trust: 0) pulls me through the door and up the stairs in Edie's wake.

The stairs end inside another crowded metro platform filled with civs and papered with wanted posters. The gang follows Edie as she leads us through the crowd as nonchalantly as possible. When we reach the street safely, air floods my lungs—sometimes you don't notice you're holding your breath until you finally inhale.

We're on the outskirts of New York. Edie leads us deftly through alleys and side streets, and we gradually make our way farther from the train station, into the city.

"Where are you taking us?" Newton says.

"A safe house," Edie says.

Nobody talks until we reach our destination, which turns out to be a trapdoor in the floor of a storage room at the back of a combination Chinese restaurant and a 24-hour laundromat.

"Fascinating," Atlas says. "How well the smells blend together—fabric softener with lo mein. It makes me hungry and sleepy all at once."

"Home sweet home."

Edie lifts the trapdoor in the storage room and shimmies down into the hole. She calls up: "Last one down, remember to close the door," and disappears once again into darkness.

Part III

People with no names, no identities. Or,
worse, puppets.
Not even human.
Toys used to satisfy the desires
of the people pulling the strings.
Except the people pulling the strings are puppets, too.

15.

Fully committing to the cause of following a stranger down a dark hole doesn't lessen the darkness of the hole. The climb down the ladder goes on for ages in the pitch black. Gradually, light creeps up from below. Finally, on the bottom rung of the ladder, it appears—the most beautiful room in the world.

In my world, anyway. Above, the two-story-high ceiling lit with enough lanterns, bulbs, chandeliers, lamps, and strings of lights to make you forget you're underground. The ladder leads down onto a paisley rug, one of many of dozens of rugs layered one on top of the other, completely covering the concrete floor. The walls, too, are camouflaged with multicolored fabric—threadbare tapestries mingle with patchwork blankets and plain old bed sheets draped to cover every inch of concrete.

The other end of the room is too far away to see, and corridors branch off on either side. It's impossible to get a real feel for how big the underground complex might actually be because every square inch is packed with people in gaudy, colorful clothes and piles of jewelry, food, electronics, and every other black-market item you'd want stacked precariously high atop carts and tables. In the nearest corner, a man wearing a pointy hat calls out, "Hot dogs! Get 'em here. Get 'em hot," while serving up the small sausages (which have been illegal since the Pork Fat Scare of 2034) from a cart. The whole place has the pungent odor of spices. Vendors are scattered all over the room, selling everything from colorful underwear and shoes to homemade flutes and guitars. Despite their over-the-top clothes, buyers and sellers alike wear no-nonsense expressions—these are people willing to fight for what they want, whether it's a bootleg copy of an ancient NAA album or a stack of credits they're rightfully owed.

"Fascinating." Atlas strokes a pair of fuzzy boots. "I haven't seen fur since I was a boy. What is this, mink?"

"Chinchilla." The vendor is a dark-haired woman not much younger than Atlas himself. "I usually sell a pair like this for three hundred credits. But I like your face, so for you, two-fifty."

"That's very flattering." Atlas reaches into his pocket.

"Don't buy those," Edie says. "They're rat fur. You can tell by the coloring."

"Mind your own business, you." The vendor and Edie get into a yelling match that looks like it might escalate to a fistfight. Instead of throwing a punch, Edie finally treats the vendor to one last insulting gesture and leads the group away, toward the back of the room, and down one of the corridors that branches off to the side. Even the hallways down here are decked out in fabric in calming shades of purple and blue.

"I'm sorry, but you have to watch out down here."

Edie pulls out a ring of old keys and unlocks a door into a small apartment, as brightly lit as the main room. A bed sits in one corner, a table and chairs in another, a stove with a bubbling pot of soup occupies a third, while a small fireplace takes up the fourth. Drawings and photos of people and animals hang all over the walls.

"Come in. Sit down." Edie goes over and stirs the pot of soup. "Dinner?"

"You live here?" It's hard to imagine anyone spending their whole life in such tight quarters.

"I do. And what's so bad about that?"

"Nothing. I . . ." It's a basement. A basement with a fireplace in the corner. "Where does the smoke go?"

"Three other apartments form a cluster with mine. All of our fireplaces meet up and vent out of one chimney. All of the chimneys in the whole basement—around two hundred—meet up with a steam vent from the sewer, and by the time it reaches the surface, our smoke is camouflaged, mixed in with the steam. Genius, isn't it?"

"If there are two hundred chimneys and each chimney vents four apartments," Cicero does the math, "then there are . . . eight hundred people that live down here?"

"Maybe three times that, I'd say. Not everyone lives alone like me. Most are families that fled the surface. They'd rather live down here than have their children taken away. That's what I mean when I say you have to be careful down here. People here are only looking out for themselves. Things are different down here than up there."

Desperate, scared people trying to hold on to what's theirs. "Doesn't sound that different."

"Well, it is." Edie searches through a small cabinet next to the stove and scrounges together five bowls and mugs. The gray-haired teen drops a spoon into each one and fills them all with steaming hot soup. "Eat."

We sit around Edie's small kitchen table while she plops onto her bed and kicks her boots off. The spicy soup feeds a hunger I didn't know was there. This underground community is the New York that was missing on that last trip to the city—a kaleidoscope of life hidden beneath bland skyrises. Clearly, Edie's presence on that train was no accident.

"Why did you bring us here?"

"You still don't trust me, huh?" Edie smiles a little. "I don't blame you. I'm not sure I trust you either. But the four of you are in some serious danger, and this basement is about the safest place on Earth you could be."

"What kind of danger?" Atlas' eyes narrow. "Are they armed?"

"Yes," Edie says.

While Atlas's expression wavers between fear and delight, Cicero simply purses her lips and says, "People with guns are after us?"

"I was on that train because I'd been in D.C. looking for you. While I was inside your apartment—"

"You broke into our loft?" Cicero says.

"For your own good. I was supposed to find you and bring you here. Well, you weren't home, so I thought I'd take a peek and see if I could find any clues about where to look for you. And while I was there, a woman in a suit came in and searched the place. A state agent, I'd guess, and not a very good one—she didn't find me."

"Great. I bet they searched our place, too." Newton's eyes go wide. "Homer!" He picks up his celly and steps into the hall to talk.

"So, you break into our apartment looking for clues but don't find any, and while you're there, an agent also breaks in, looking for clues, and doesn't find any. The agent leaves, then you leave, and you happen to find yourself in the same train car as us?"

"Exactly. And when I heard you talking, I knew who you were, so I extracted you."

"Who told you to . . . extract . . . us?" For a civ, Edie seems to know a lot about the state and police-work.

"Heloise wants you here, and she sent me to find you. Well, *she* didn't. She sent someone to send someone to send me to find you. Come to think of it, I don't think she's ever even set foot down here."

"Heloise? We were on our way to find her. Does she know Atlas is with us?"

"She doesn't even know I've found you, yet. News takes a little while to travel to the surface. It's like the smoke in that way. And like I said, Heloise doesn't spend too much time in the basement, so it'll be a while before she even knows you're here."

"Good." That gives us some time. "Seems to me the rebels have two leaders—Heloise and Atlas. Heloise wants to go through the proper channels and get rid of the WI by manipulating the government to her advantage. Atlas wants to overthrow the WI by force. I'm not sure either of those options will work. What if the politicians take our money and vote to make NAA illegal anyway? What if we go after the WI with guns, and we all get killed?"

"So what do you suggest we do? Nothing?"

"I'm saying that Heloise and Atlas have come up with these two solutions on their own, without consulting anybody. We've got a good chance to find out what actual rebels think. You said yourself there are thousands of people down here. Well, what if one of them has an idea?"

"Darwin's right," Cicero says. "Elections and wars are the ways people got things done in the past. Sorry, Mr. Atlas."

"No, no, my dear. Don't apologize," Atlas says. "I admit I'm a bit out of touch."

Newton comes back in the room, the panic gone from his face. "Homer's fine. He hasn't seen anything, but I told him to go ahead and come to New York."

"Okay then." Looks like National Selection's going to be making another appearance in New York. "Edie, can we get some people together?"

"A party!" Newton says.

"Not a party. A rally. And you want to do this as soon as possible, I assume?" Edie goes out and knocks on the door across the hall. A boy of about nine or ten answers, wearing a pair of red corduroy pants that are too big and a red sweater that's too small.

"Hey, Edie."

"Hey, Mouse. We need everyone in the common hall ASAP. Can you get the word out?"

"Sure thing. Is it an emergency?"

"Yeah. Now go!"

Mouse lets the door slam behind him as he takes off running down the corridor, banging on doors and screaming as loud as he can, "Everyone to the common hall! Emergency meeting! Emergency!!!"

"Why do you call that little boy Mouse?" Atlas smiles as he watches the boy run through the halls.

"Because he's quiet as a mouse," Edie says.

"Is that supposed to be ironic?" Cicero says. "The kid named Mouse is loud but real mice are quiet."

"Not down here. Basement mice. Rats, really. They're huge. You can hear them all hours of the night, running around through the sewer ducts."

"Gross."

Edie leads us back through the winding corridors toward the common room, the room with the ladder to the surface. Vendors push their carts aside to make room for the crowd beginning to gather. Edie goes to the end of the room, where a small plywood stage is piled with junk, and moves a stack of empty soy milk crates, leaving room to stand between a discarded couch and some broken ceiling fans.

"I know it's not what you're used to, and we don't have a mic, so you'll have to yell."

"It's fine."

Except there's a nervous twinge in my belly that hasn't showed up since my first recital at age five. Thousand of performances for thousands of people without thinking twice, but now, standing up on a rarely used plywood stage in a spruced-up basement—now the nerves show up? This is different; tonight is a discussion—no hamming it up in the spotlight. There's no chance to impress the crowd with vibrato or falsetto. My ideas will have to do all the work. Darwin's Rule #56 (a new one)—The Message Is More Important Than the Messenger.

"Hi, I'm Darwin—"

Someone yells, "What's she saying?" and another person chimes in, "Yell loud, girl!"

"I'm Darwin Singer. I'm a member of the band National Selection."

A few people cheer.

"I'm here to talk with you about the WI and NAA. As you probably know, I work for the WI."

A few people boo.

"But I am a rebel, too. Right now, NAA isn't illegal. Not officially. But the WI wants to change that."

A lot of people boo.

"And the rebels are fighting back. We've got one set of rebels planning to talk the government into removing the regulations on art. We've got another set of rebels who would rather take up arms and fight the WI—stage a full-on revolution. I think the system won't work. Violence isn't the answer either. I propose to you that there may be a third option. And I want you to tell me what that third option is. What should we do? What do you think?"

"Move to Canada!" Someone says, and a few people laugh.

The crowd falls silent for a few moments, as if they expect me to keep talking. But I don't. I wait. And the crowd starts to murmur. Soon, those murmurs turn to whispers, and those whispers to words, and those words to shouts, so that everyone is yelling all at once.

"One at a time!"

An older woman with white hair raises her hand in the back of the room. The crowd quiets down to listen to her speak.

"What if we try to do without NAA? I'm tired of living underground. I want to go outside!"

Several people shout agreement. Many people boo.

"You go ahead and surrender to the fascists, Granny. We don't need you down here!"

A young woman near the front of the crowd pumps her fist in the air. She nearly punches the man next to her.

"I say we fight! Beat 'em senseless!"

"We're trying to come up with a new idea. Voting and fighting surely aren't the only options, are they?"

"I have an idea."

A young man makes his way toward the front of the crowd, people stepping aside to let him pass. When he steps on stage next to me, it's clear that he's just about my height—maybe even shorter. Impressive that such a small man can command that much respect from the crowd.

"They call me Gates. As in Bill. I'm kind of a computer freak." He shakes my hand and turns to the crowd. "What if we do exactly what Granny said? We go above ground."

"You want us all to go to jail?"

"Hear me out," Gates says. "I've been thinking about this for a while. Even if the legislation passes, possession of NAA won't be illegal. As proposed, the law won't let them arrest us for what we do on private property. They're trying to make performing in public and selling art illegal. So, the answer is two-fold. First, we give the art away. Free concerts, free media drives full of art, free everything. Giving it away doesn't violate the law. And since our music and art are better than the WI's, people will stop buying from the WI, and they'll go out of business. Second, we form private clubs and hold our concerts and art shows on private property. We limit membership and charge dues, like a fraternity. We don't break any laws—we don't do anything wrong. The state can't touch us."

The crowd begins shouting all at once, some approvingly, some disapprovingly, but all at top volume. Gates simply steps off the stage and makes his way back into the crowd.

"We have an idea." A good one—go above ground; do everything legally, right in front of their faces. "Does anybody have any thoughts on where we should start?"

"Let's start with the club." Cicero steps onto the stage. "What are the membership criteria?"

"You can't be an employee of the WI!"

"Now, wait a minute." Newton joins us on stage. "We're, all three of us, WI employees."

"To get in," says the young woman in front of the stage, "all applicants must produce one work of non-approved art."

"That's a good one. What else?"

"You have to show up in non-approved clothes!"

"Perfect." Cicero rapidly takes notes. "Each city will have it's own chapter, and each chapter will have weekly meetings located on some piece of private property."

"Meanwhile, we'll record and distribute music for free." National Selection's already halfway there.

"We'll publish novels and hand them out on the street," Cicero says.

The crowd cheers.

"And what makes you think all this will work?" Atlas joins us on stage. "You have to take power by force. It's the only way real change ever happens."

"Untrue." Gates shouts over the crowd. "What about the invention of the interweb? That was a revolution in information. And when we figured out how to use water as fuel? That was a revolution in technology. Change doesn't have to be violent."

The crowd roars its approval.

"I can see I'm outnumbered."

Atlas steps back off the stage. Newton gives him a pat on the shoulder, but Atlas simply sits down on a crate next to the stage.

"I know there are some of you who are skeptical, and I can't change your minds for you. All I'm asking is that you give us a chance. Make your art. Give it away for free. And if we really don't make a difference, if nothing really changes, then . . ." I can't bear to say it, but the end of that sentence in my head is, "we've failed." What I actually say is "we'll try something else."

Not much of a motivational speaker, am I? No matter. We've got an idea almost guaranteed to work. But, as the crowd breaks up into smaller groups, people leaving the common room, the one potential flaw in the plan becomes clear. What if, after the music's made, no one wants to hear it? Sure, there are thousands of rebels nationwide, but for this plan to succeed, we'll have to up our number to millions. What if people don't want to watch movies or see ballets? What if there's just no interest in reading about fictional worlds or looking at abstract art? What if this is all for nothing?

16.

This is the part where we try and convince the most powerful, greediest woman in the rebel movement to give music away for free. At this point, it seems just as likely that aliens will land right here outside the combination Chinese restaurant and 24-hour laundromat and declare Earth a condemned planet. The limo pulls away from the curb stuffed with a few rebels, a handful of WI defectors and a white-haired real-estate tycoon, but between all of us, we can't muster up enough confidence in the task ahead to even make idle chatter during the drive to SFL headquarters for our meeting with Heloise. The silence in the car only amplifies the sound of my rumbling stomach—hopefully it's nerves and not Edie's soup turning on me. This meeting with Heloise is sure to be rough. What can she actually do, though, if she doesn't agree with the private-club, free-music plan?

"She'll turn us all in," Cicero says, once again displaying her uncanny ability to say exactly what everyone else is trying not to think about.

"No, she can't," Newton says. "That's the beauty of this plan. We won't be doing anything illegal."

"They arrested Croon, and he wasn't doing anything illegal."

"Yeah but they let him go after what, three or four nights in jail?"

"Three or four nights in jail is three or four nights too many," Cicero says.

"Agreed." And if they find out we actually are doing something illegal, that three or four nights could turn into a lifetime rotting away in Phase II. "We have to come up with an escape plan."

"Here's a plan," Homer says. "When the cops show up, we run like hell."

"Here's an even better plan," Atlas says. "How about we don't go to Heloise at all? I don't trust her. You don't need her to get this plan started."

He's right, of course, but it would be nice to have at least one competent adult on our side. Atlas doesn't exactly fit the description.

"If something feels wrong, if one of us sees something or hears something or even senses something out of the ordinary, we signal the others, and we calmly leave, immediately."

Homer huffs. "Like I said. We run like hell."

The conversation dies down as the limo pulls up to the SFL headquarters building. Once everyone piles out, we stand on the sidewalk for a second before going inside, almost like we're taking a collective deep breath before diving into the deep end.

On each either side of the doorway to Heloise's office hang photos of the woman with various famous people—Heloise and the current SFL champs; Heloise and Copernicus Player, handsome star of an Oscar-winning history about Napoleon and Josephine; Heloise and the liberal senator from New York. Dozens of similar pictures hang inside the office, too, intermingled with small statues and busts of historic figures she must've brought back from her travels around the world—it seems the morality director collects sculptures as well as powerful friends. Heloise sits behind her desk at the far end of the room, underneath the bust of an ancient president, her fingers tented, smiling a wide smile that looks more threatening than happy.

"Come in," Heloise calls. "How was the trip?"

"Good to be back in New York." D.C. seems far away and small compared to New York's in-your-face big-ness. Unfortunately, that big-ness makes *everything* seem small, including me, us, and our little rebellion.

Heloise leans back in her chair. "Good to see you all here. Kids. Atlas. Shame it has to be under such unfortunate circumstances—armed agents chasing after you and all. I apologize for having to put you up in the basement. That place can be a little . . . musty and dank, but it's secure. We can't have you staying in hotels—too public. Edie, I trust you showed them their quarters?"

"Yes."

The rest of us agree, too, though we haven't been shown a single thing except Edie's tiny apartment and the common room full of people. Keeping the rally secret seems best.

"And are the accommodations satisfactory?"

"Quite," Atlas says. "Quite cozy in fact."

"Good," Heloise says. "You won't be staying there long, anyway."

"We won't?" Newton says.

"No," Heloise says. "You'll be on tour. Remember?"

"About that . . ." Time to break the news. "We're not going."

"Excuse me?" Heloise gives me the same look she might give a child who insists he'll never eat another vegetable in his life.

"I—We don't want to."

"Afraid, are you? Well, don't worry. I've got a security network strong enough and well-funded enough to protect you from groupies, state agents, and the apocalypse if necessary."

"It's not that. We . . . think there might be another way to fight the WI."

Heloise's disapproving gaze lands on Atlas. He stares back at her, unintimidated.

"Another way? His way? You want to charge the capital with machetes and trebuchets? Ha! You might as well turn yourselves in to Phase II." Heloise looks like she regrets saying the words as soon as they come out of her mouth.

"What do you know about Phase II?"

"Never mind Phase II. Attacking the WI is suicide."

"Tell us everything."

Heloise sighs. "It's not what you think it is—it's not a prison. It's a top-secret research facility run by the WI. The research varies, but last I heard they were developing psychological techniques to change a person's behavior permanently. To make a lazy person energetic, for example. Or a sloppy person neat. Turning non-approved traits into approved ones."

Actually, that sounds pretty much *exactly* like a prison. "And where is Phase II? Denver? St. Louis?"

"D.C."

"Where in D.C.? Is my father there?"

"I don't know," Heloise says. "What I do know is none of us want to end up there. So, give up this crazy revolution idea."

"They already have," says Atlas. "And so have I. We've laid down our arms."

"What's he talking about?"

Atlas's celly rings. "Brax."

"Don't pick up," Homer says. "He's working for the state, remember? They can use the phone call to track where you are."

"He's right," Edie says. "When we get back to the basement, give me your phones. Between Gates and I, we should be able to make you untraceable."

"You can do that?" Cicero says.

"They don't call me Edison for nothing."

"What, exactly, am I missing?" Heloise says. "You say you're not going on tour, and that you're not planning to attack the WI. So are you giving up?"

Newton points toward the sky. "We're taking the whole operation above ground, so to speak."

"What Newton means is that we plan to do everything— write music, print books, and have concerts—right under the WI's nose. Think about it. What are they actually making illegal?"

"The sale of non-approved art," says Heloise.

"Exactly. So, we give it away."

"Performing non-approved art in public places will be illegal, too," Heloise says.

"So, we set up private clubs on private property. We won't be breaking any laws."

"The WI will change the laws."

"The WI can't change the laws if the WI doesn't exist," Cicero says. "If there's good art available—and I think all of us will agree that even the worst non-approved art is better than the crap we're used to making at the WI. If good art is available, people won't want the other stuff. They'll stop buying from the WI, and the WI will go out of business. And if the WI goes out of business—"

"No one will be pushing the government to regulate art," says Heloise.

"But we need your help. Those recordings you made of us, that you were planning to sell. We need you to give those out for free."

"No."

Heloise walks around her desk to a large cabinet and pulls a media drive off a shelf.

"If the WI goes out of business . . . If the state doesn't change the laws . . . Too many ifs. Besides, I'm a businesswoman, and giving product away for free is not good business. But, I won't stop you." She places the media drive in my hand. "This contains everything we recorded. Do what you want. But if it doesn't work—"

"It will work." Maybe if I say it enough times, I'll convince myself, too. Darwin's Rule #9—Believe Your Lines.

"But if it doesn't work," Heloise continues, "we need a plan B. We're still doing the tour without you. If the time comes when we need the money to grease some palms in D.C.—"

"We won't need to."

"We'll be ready just in case," Heloise says. "Maybe between all of us, we can make this happen."

"Can we still count on that security you promised us?" Newton says.

"Absolutely." Heloise walks us out the door and toward the elevator. "As long as you're in New York, you're safe. Too bad I can't say the same for D.C."

It is too bad. Especially since knowing Phase II is somewhere in D.C. makes it impossible to not go back. My father is there—he's been there forever, right under my nose, being experimented on, tortured. Have they managed to change him with their "psychological research" in all these years? Have they beaten the rebel out of him?

Rush-hour traffic has picked up, and we sit idling in the limo as civs on hydrobikes blow past us, their socks pulled up over their pants. New York is just as much of a rebel city as D.C., but it doesn't quite feel like home.

"You're thinking about heading back to D.C.?" Atlas says.

"Not thinking about it," Cicero says. "She's planning on it. I can tell."

"You're insane," Homer says. "They'll arrest you if they find you."

"I know I shouldn't go back. You know that I have to."

"Not now, though, right?" Newton says. "Now, we have work to do. Here, in New York."

Handing out media drives, printing novels, scouting club locations, swearing in members . . . Yes, there's plenty of work to do in New York. But there's some thinking to do, too. How exactly do you go about discovering the location of a top-secret research lab? And once you discover the lab's location, how do you get in?

The basement's in the middle of a full-blown party by the time we get back. Folks dance, sing, and work on the pieces of NAA they need to join the New York chapter of the private rebel club. Mouse is writing a haiku about life underground. The fur vendor ponders a sketch of a half-rat, half-boot creature. A set of instruments appeared on stage while we were gone. Dozens of the "Wanted: National

Selection" fliers are pinned to the fabric on the wall behind it.

"I take it someone wants us to perform," Homer says.

"We may be a lot of things down here," Edie says. "Loud, smelly, soggy . . . But one thing we're not is subtle."

As usual, it takes some persuasion to get Cicero to join in, but when she finally takes hold of her tambourine, the band feels complete—as complete as it can be without Franklin. The mic, a large, ornate thing, swings down from the ceiling, straight out of an old movie. The crowd cheers.

"As happy as National Selection is to be here with you tonight in your lovely underground utopia, we're even happier to report that this, my friends, will be the last show we ever play in a basement! We'd like to dedicate this performance to Franklin Keys, keyboardist and political prisoner."

It's not easy to sleep on a hard cot, in a strange bed, underground. Contrary to all the colorful stories about mice Edie told us, the basement is actually very quiet at night—too quiet. The underground's damp silence is worse than the cold, concrete quiet of the WI dorms. These days, I fall asleep to the noise of the Atlas District: the groans and creaks of the loft's wood floors shifting in the night, the laughter of civs on the streets below floating in through the cracks around the windows. The place has its own sort of music.

It isn't silence that's really the problem, though. The quiet doesn't help, but an image—maybe a moment of a dream—keeps playing again and again in my head: me, alone on stage, behind a microphone, singing, skin wrinkled, voice thin and raspy. Like Atlas, I've grown old fighting against the WI, and despite my best efforts, I'm still stuck hiding in basements, fighting the good fight, skin wrinkled, hair wispy and white as the cobwebs in the corners.

Maybe a walk through a few winding corridors will help. Cicero manages to stay asleep as the door of the small apartment we're sharing opens and closes silently. Out in the hall, the lights are dimmed, too. The common room seems even bigger now that it's dark and empty.

"Hello."

"Hello," comes the faint echo back.

Beyond the makeshift stage, there's a corridor on the other side. This side of the basement looks much the same as the rest—faceless halls with door after door after door. Even after walking for a while, there's no shaking the nagging image. But thankfully, exhaustion is creeping in.

A turn in the direction that should lead back to the apartment instead winds up at a dead end. Another direction, another dead end. Around another corner, and prepared to meet my third dead end in a row, I instead come face-to-face with a massive wooden door. If the door leads to the surface, it'll be easy to get back to the combination Chinese restaurant and 24-hour laundromat, through the trap door, and back into the common room. From there, getting back to the room'll be easy.

The worn slab of wood resists, but with a serious tug, the door groans open just enough for me to slide past it and discover that it doesn't lead to a set of stairs to the surface. Instead, a large room comes into view, dark near the door, but lit at the opposite end by a bright, flickering light. The room smells of smoke and as I head toward the light, the shape of a fireplace emerges, and in front of it, a large upholstered chair, its back to me. Apart from the occasional crackle of a log on the fire, silence fills the room. Until, that is, a sigh comes from the chair. Approach or go back out the door?

"Friend or foe?" A girl's voice.

"I was wondering the same thing. Do you know the way back to the living quarters?"

"Course I do," the girl says. "You lost?"

Once my eyes adjust to the light from the fire, the girl's face becomes clear—Edie. I'm not the only restless rebel tonight.

"I couldn't sleep."

The floor in front of the chair is piled with pillows and cushions that look so comfortable that I just sit down, choosing immediate comfort in place of wandering back to bed. Edie's eyes look puffy and red, like she's been crying, but before I can ask if she's okay, she speaks.

"I used to be in the WI."

The gray-haired girl did look familiar at first on the train. We were probably in the same year for a while—maybe even had some of the same classes. Of course, her hair wouldn't have been gray back then. The dye-job is a new addition.

"Those drawings on your walls: You did those?"

"I did. I was a painter, and a dancer, and a woodwind player. I did it all at first. And when it came time for me to choose, I couldn't . . . even when they punished me. One day in oboe class, I started tapping my foot to help me keep the beat, and the instructor came over and stood on my foot. Keeping the beat is what drummers do, not little girls who play oboe. I couldn't have been more than eight years old, and a grown man had his full weight on my foot. It hurt so bad I had to stop playing. Three broken bones. But I wouldn't cry. I refused. Just like I refused to choose a discipline. I ran away before they could kick me out."

You hear about initiates taking a little time to decide which form of art they'll practice, but you never hear of anyone refusing to choose. Knowing what I now know about the WI, their methods of enforcing their rules, however harsh, aren't surprising.

"And that's when you came here?"

"I lived on the streets for a while . . . You didn't know D.C. had homeless people, did you? This underground network of artists isn't the only underground network in the world, you know. Anyway, a family found me digging through a refuse bin for food and took me in. Mouse's family—he was just a baby, then. When he got older and started to draw, I told the family what I knew about the WI and what I had heard about this place, and we came here."

"And you don't live with them anymore?"

"I got my own room—didn't want to be a burden."

"What about your birth family?"

"What about them? They sent me away. They didn't come visit once."

"What if they had no choice? What if they were afraid? You saw firsthand what the WI can do. My father—"

"They may as well be dead." As soon as Edie says the words, she puts her hand over her mouth as if trying to stop them before they escape. "I'm sorry, I didn't mean that."

Silence fills the room as the fire dies down.

"You heard my sob story. I'm sitting in here alone in the dark crying because someone stepped on my toe. What's your problem?"

"I guess I'm worried about making things happen. Or not making anything happen."

"Who put you in charge?"

Who had? Atlas made a point to tell me I'm not important to the revolution. Heloise certainly sees no need for me. So, who?

"Nobody, I guess. Nobody but myself."

"Sounds like you think too much."

"I've never been accused of *that* before."

"Granny—you remember, the old woman from the rally—she told me a proverb once. Don't know who said it first—a philosopher, a preacher . . . But if you find yourself procrastinating, afraid, then you're supposed to look at yourself in the mirror and say, 'Just do it.' Overcome your fear. Don't think; act. Granny remembered it from her childhood, said it used to be kind of a religious thing—a chant. You say it to yourself over and over again. That's my first rule of survival—just do it."

"Just do it."

Can it really be that easy? All it will take to locate Phase II, find my father, and bring down the WI is to just . . . do it?

"Thinking again, aren't you? You know what I think (now you've got *me* thinking). You should sit up with me for a little while and watch the fire—no thinking allowed."

17.

Giving music away is more difficult than it sounds. New York has become the flagship location for the free art agenda, but reports from the field suggest the world might not be ready for rebels on parade. A string quartet spends all Saturday playing on a subway platform, watching people get on the wrong train rather than be caught listening to classical music. A mime is followed around Times Square by a heckler yelling profanities that would have gotten him arrested had the police not been yelling along with him. A group of teenagers douses a fire-breather with chocolate shakes. An ad (paid for by Atlas) on the Private Library's massive media screens proclaims art to be a right, not a crime, but even Newton's face smiling down on the Pleasure District makes no difference. People are too afraid to look or to listen.

Heading out into a park with Newton and Cicero in tow has become a morning ritual. Cicero hands out media drives filled with music, books, movies, and art while Newton and I perform. Cicero's role always goes well at first—people love to get their hands on anything free, even something as cheap as a media drive. But when the music starts up, any crowd that's gathered scatters.

Today's no different. The weather is warmer than it has been, newly budding leaves tremble in a warm breeze, and people are everywhere—sunning on blankets spread on the grass, jogging, picnicking—but they all flee Newton's guitar and my voice as if we're police sirens signaling an impending raid.

"We'll never get anybody into our music this way," Newton says.

"Sure we will."

"How?" Cicero says. "They're running from us."

"They're running from Newton and me. Not from you. We'll stay here and keep performing. You go get as far away from us as possible and hand out the media drives to anyone who'll take one. And people are taking them, right? Even after you tell them what's on it?"

"Well . . . I figured people would be more likely to take them if they didn't know. And when they plug them in and find the NAA in their own homes, alone . . . I think they'll like what they see." Cicero heads across the park.

"I'll go find a different spot, too. Maybe if we split up, people won't feel so threatened." Newton takes his guitar and trots off.

You're not supposed to sit while singing—it distorts the voice—but we're way past breaking simple rules here, so there's no reason not to get comfy on the concrete edge of a fountain. Who's here to hear it, anyway? My eyes drift closed for a moment to block out the glare of the sun on the water, and when I open them, there's a little girl standing nearby, staring at me. Listening.

She can't be more than five or six, but by that age, even civilian children have been taught about NAA and its "dangers." Yet here she is, standing with her little hands shoved in the pockets of her gray dress, listening. I smile at her. The girl smiles back. A man sitting on a bench looks up from the newspaper he's been reading. A jogger slows as she passes. Others nearby begin to take notice.

"Where's the girl's mother?"

"Should we do something?"

"It's not our place."

"If that was my child—"

"If either of them were my child . . ."

It's time to stand up and put on a show. A small crowd has gathered. This calls for a little dancing, too. The crowd's murmurs grow louder—one person even boos. But no one turns away. As if on cue, Newton walks up, picks up the tune and starts strumming. Even more people stop to watch. Cicero comes over and hands out media drives to people too mesmerized by the performance to notice what they've been given. The song ends with a now-familiar sight—a silent crowd.

"Well, how does it feel?"

No one answers, so I get up close to the first row of onlookers.

"You've experienced something you've never seen before in your entire lives."

There's the jogger who stopped to listen.

"How does it feel?"

The jogger runs away. There's the man who's been reading the newspaper. He tucks the newspaper under his arm and shuffles off. The little girl who was the first to listen.

"What's your name?"

"Melody," the little girl says.

"Huh, that used to be my name. My name's Darwin, now. I'm named after a famous scientist. What made you come over and listen to my song?"

The little girl says nothing.

"Do you sing, too?"

The little girl closes her eyes and begins to sing softly, a song about all the butterflies she can see from her bedroom window. Her voice is nice, if untrained, and the tune is simple; Newton begins to strum along.

Success! We reached one person. A huge victory, even if she is a tiny girl. The memory of sitting on the metro listening to real music for the first time floods back to me like a fire igniting, followed quickly by memories of my early days as a prisoner of the WI—darkness.

"How has the WI not snatched you up?"

A man shoves his way through the crowd, not bothering to give out even a "'scuse me."

"Melanie!"

He grabs the little girl and carries her away.

"Stay away from my daughter."

The silent crowd clears. People return to their picnics and sunbathing.

"Score one for us."

"One down," Newton says.

"And four hundred ninety-nine million nine hundred ninety-nine thousand nine hundred ninety-nine to go," Cicero says. "Do you think her father will be able to keep the WI away from her?"

"No." As sure as that girl's name was Melody and not Melanie, it's even more sure that the little girl, whatever her name is, will soon become another censored voice.

You could spend all day writing new songs in the basement's only really warm room, the one with the big wooden door and huge fireplace—the rebels call it the living room. Often, small two- or three-person songwriting meetings turn into twenty-person jam sessions or full-fledged parties. Acrobats, fortune-tellers and comedians—they all come to sit in and play, listen, or brainstorm. An NAA historian (a man in a top hat) brings in hundreds of pages of hundred-year-old preserved sheet music, and Newton and a group of violinists and cellists disappear to set up a makeshift recording studio in an abandoned root cellar and resurrect some dead composers.

No news about Heloise lately. That can't be a good sign. How's the tour? Has the state put a stop to it? Are they really making enough money to influence politicians? The folks in the basement deserve to know. So whenever Atlas finds his way to the living room (he usually passes the time sitting in the corner of the Chinese restaurant upstairs, reading the newspaper and sipping wonton soup), he's bombarded with questions. The lack of interweb in the basement means Atlas, with his old-fashioned paper newspapers, is the only one around who bothers keeping up with the outside world.

"What's the word on Heloise?" As much as Atlas despises her, he'll surely be on the lookout for news about the tour.

"Heloise?"

Atlas has taken to wearing his pajamas all the time again. And he's become more and more disoriented since we started living in the basement. That's why he goes upstairs so often, despite the danger of being spotted. The dark isn't good for his mind, he says. Old age needs the light.

"Your sworn enemy . . . The woman who wants to lock you away so she can run the revolution herself."

"Ah, yes. No word in the papers about her. Don't worry, my dear. What's that old saying? 'No news is good news.' Nothing being said about Heloise and her tour means that the state hasn't found out about her roving bands of outlaws. No, I suspect they're carrying on fine. There is word, however, on my son."

He pulls a newspaper clipping (ripping, actually—he'd torn the story right out of the page) from the pocket of his pajama pants. A picture of Brax, smiling and wearing a suit, standing next to a newly erected statue of himself in front of the Atlas Theatre. The giant headline: "Atlas Dead, Atlas Takes Over."

"You don't look dead."

"I don't feel dead, either. I have a bit of an upset stomach—basement food—but nothing serious enough to end me."

According to the article, when Atlas (the elder) disappeared, Brax took over as acting president of Atlas Realty. After an appropriate amount of time passed (two weeks), Brax had his father declared dead and then became official president of Atlas Realty. His first order of business was to tear down his father's statue and erect a new one (of himself) in its place. Next, he plans to liquidate all of Atlas Realty's properties that aren't making enough money. He'll sell every last building in the Atlas District, which the article quotes him as calling "an eyesore—an embarrassing opposition to both progress and the state's authority."

"I guess we finally know whose side he's on." The rat—he's worse than the villains in gangster films. At least those guys are loyal to one side.

"I don't understand why." Atlas plops down in the armchair in front of the fire and puts his head in his hands. "I gave him everything."

"We won't let him do it. We'll stop him."

"How can we, when we're stuck down here in this mouse hole?"

"We'll go back to D.C. How long do you think we have to stop him before it's too late?"

"A month, at most. If he's already got buyers lined up, two weeks."

"We'll do it in one." It's time we talked about the card printed with Atlas's initials. I hand the card to Atlas. "My mother gave me this."

"My old calling card. I haven't seen one of these in years. Your father's?"

"You worked with my father, and you never bothered to tell me before now?"

"It didn't come up."

It takes every bit of willpower not to grab Atlas by the shoulders and shake him. This isn't the time for jokes.

"Your father and I met in the very café where you and I first met. He was young, then, and so was I—younger, anyway. We realized we had a lot in common and struck up a friendship. We planned to take down the WI. We didn't know how, but we knew we had to, for your sake, and for Brax's."

"Sounds like you were close."

"We were. We'd only just begun planning, building our army, but, after my wife's death—the first in a string of 'accidents' I suspect were perpetrated by the WI. I couldn't . . . You just get sick of losing people."

"So you locked yourself away and gave up on fighting the WI, even though your wife would have wanted the revolt to continue. Even though my father kept on fighting."

"Selfish, I admit, but if I hadn't gone into hiding, I don't think I'd be here today. Self-preservation is mankind's most valuable instinct. Your father might still be around if—"

"Mankind has survived this long because we evolved empathy, compassion. We help each other. My father could've used your help."

"There are a lot of things about my past that I regret. I did everything I could to help your father, but he was stubborn and arrogant. He was sure his way was the right way, and he couldn't see the danger ahead. Or he just wouldn't listen."

"You thought the WI had something to do with his accident?"

"I was almost positive that your father and my wife were victims of some treacherous conspiracy. But I had no proof. We had no proof, so your mother and I had to do what we could to keep you and Brax safe. I gave up fighting. She gave up her daughter."

Atlas' wide mouth sags at the corners with the weight of the past. My vision goes blurry as moisture fills my eyes. There are no more answers to give, but a single question still hangs in the air. How can I succeed where others failed before me?

The exodus from New York is almost as abrupt as our rough entry into life in the basement. We say a few goodbyes on the way out, but Cicero thinks it best not to make a big deal out of our departure.

Wanted posters still plaster the trains, but by now most have been covered with other signs. They still flash across the screens, but less often—the 24-hour news networks have found more interesting stories. It doesn't matter, anyway. As a parting gift, Edie found a woman to give Natural Selection makeovers. My curls now shine bright red, Cicero has short brown hair, and Newton sports a mohawk.

When we get to D.C., it's straight for the safe house. As much as Newton begs to sleep in his own bed, and Cicero pleads to go home and water her houseplants, it can't happen. Our homes are being watched. And our parents' homes. And our friends'. There's no proof of the surveillance, but I've watched enough old crime dramas to know that when the government comes after you, your life isn't your own anymore.

The train ride into town is a dismal affair, with everyone fretting over where to go. Atlas finally chimes in.

"I know a place."

"We've already ruled out your office," Cicero says. "Too obvious."

"It's a house out in the suburbs. My house."

"We appreciate the offer, Mr. Atlas," says Cicero, "but if you own it, the state knows about it—they have records for that type of thing."

"Not in this case. We never registered the deed with the city. My wife Gina paid for the house in cash."

"Really?"

"I was poor when we married, and her family was wealthy . . . and corrupt. Their sympathies lied too closely with the state, in her opinion. So she bought the house in secret—paid cash so her family wouldn't know about it. Our own house. Our little piece of the world, away from her family. We lived there for the first few years of Brax's life—he was too young to remember. But when she died—a severe case of food poisoning, they say—I began to hate the place. Life in the suburbs felt too still without her. She was a painter . . . I moved into the office building, into the city. The house is still there, I presume, though I haven't been back."

No one says anything for a few moments. A story this wild takes time to sink in.

Cicero finally speaks up. "That's a very sad story, Mr. Atlas, but I don't believe it. You say you were dirt poor, but you're an Atlas. You belong the most powerful family in D.C. The story can't be true. He's trying to lure us out into the suburbs, into a trap."

"I should've explained. When we married, my name was Martin Walstaff. Her father wanted a son but had only daughters. My wife was the oldest, and the first to get married, so I agreed to change my name. I became the next Atlas so that when our son, Brax, was born, he, the real Atlas heir, could carry on the family name."

"She was the Atlas, and you changed your name." Maybe the man does have a sense of compassion—he certainly seems to care about his wife.

"I'm so sorry I accused you," Cicero says. "I had no idea."

"You wouldn't. Most of the people who knew about it are dead, and the ones that aren't don't care. The rest of the Atlas sisters felt the same way about their father as Gina did—more so. When they married, they took their husbands' names, moved away, and considered themselves Atlas refugees."

By now we've reached the metro's end. We walk, once again, through the suburbs, this time led by the elder Atlas. He winds his way around corner after corner. Each intersection seems the same, each street as empty as the last. Finally, we reach the house. No mistaking it—the same concrete cube as the rest of them, but the lawn has gone to seed. No longer a perfect square of grass, the yard has sprouted full of tiny blue flowers. It's hard to resist the urge to take a picture with my celly, but pretty flowers aren't reason enough to provide the state any clues about this location.

"Weeds." Atlas leads us through the front gate. "We couldn't keep them out of the yard. Brax would pick them and make bouquets for Gina. She'd wear them in her hair, even though they smelled like rotten soymilk." Atlas unlocks the front door, and turns on the lights—the fluorescent bulbs take a while, but soon buzz to life. "Place hasn't been occupied in over ten years."

"What about your neighbors? Won't they notice the lights?" The neighbor's living room is in plain view from Atlas's window.

"The whole point of living out here is so you don't ever have to

149

talk to your neighbors." Atlas pulls tarps off furniture, exposing plush couches identical to the ones in his office. "Martians could move in next door and the neighbors would make a point to ignore the spaceship. Or maybe they'll figure Brax sold the place."

"Should we cut the grass?" Newton's been staring out the front window at the lawn.

Cicero elbows him in the ribs. "I think we should spend as little time outside as possible. Don't you, Mr. Atlas?" But Atlas has already disappeared into one of the bedrooms and shut the door. "Nice work, Newton. The man's clearly having a hard time, and you suggest we rip up the flowers in the front yard that remind him of his dead wife?"

"I'm being practical here." Newton steps away from the window. "I appreciate that he's upset, but our lives are in danger. We can't afford for one of these white-picket-fence types to rat us out." Newton finds a second bedroom to shut himself into.

"He's been watching too many gangster movies." Cicero finds a third.

The house is filled with dust-covered, framed family photos of Atlas, Brax and his mother. Does Brax really not remember living here? If he doesn't, it means the group can stay here safely, but it also means he has no memory of his mother. We're the same then—both missing a parent, both taken away from home at a young ago to start life over, both unaware of the part we were to play in a war even our parents couldn't have known we'd fight.

18.

A shrill beeping. Another rude awakening. Smoke burns my nose. Fire. I spring to my feet, determined to reach the others and get everyone out before the flames spread.

Then—laughter? The voices and the beeping are coming from house's kitchen.

Atlas fans the smoke away from a pan full of burnt French toast, and there's Edie, already gathering ingredients to have another go at it. Cicero flings open a window, and Gates deactivates the smoke detector. Even Mouse is sneaking around, quietly snatching scraps from the pans that haven't yet caught fire.

"Morning." Newton hands me a cup of coffee. "We weren't gonna wake you until breakfast was done."

Edie gives me the sugar and cream. "You didn't think we'd miss our chance to have a go at the WI, did you? You don't get to have all the fun."

"I'm glad you're here, but I don't know how much fun this'll be. I don't even know where to start."

Atlas loads the table down with heaping dishes of food. "My best ideas come when I'm eating." A mouthful of eggs doesn't stop him from talking. "Now, I didn't risk arrest shopping for groceries in my pajamas this morning so you could all just stand there and stare at me. Go on, sit down."

"Where do we start? With the next step of our plan, I mean." Giving art away wasn't a total failure, but it wasn't a success either. We need to try something new.

"It seems to me that before you begin, you need to know what your ultimate goal is. So, what's the ultimate goal?" Edie looks around the table, waiting for answers.

Cicero speaks up. "We want the government to stop enforcing the WI's decency standards, including the dress codes."

"Wait," says Newton, "the dress codes are the WI's doing, too?"

"I stayed up late last night doing some research. I've written a report on my findings if anyone would like to read it." Cicero plops a stack of papers onto the table.

"So, the WI's the reason girls can't wear short skirts?" Newton says. "Bastards."

"Guess who owns a chain of approved clothing stores—the highest-grossing chain in the country." Cicero points to the proof on the top sheet of her research.

"The WI is everywhere. The way I see it we have three options." Gates grabs an empty chair and joins the conversation. "Option one—disable the WI by killing its income. Heloise is trying to do that. Even if she succeeds in crippling the music arm of their empire, they still have the clothes—"

"And food." Cicero flips the pages of her report. "Who do you think is behind the new healthy-eating regulations? The WI has a hand in nearly every industry in the country. Art, clothes, food. It doesn't stop there. They're pushing the state to privatize prison, school, and healthcare. They want to control everything—to *sell* everything."

Gates gives Cicero's research a quick look. "Option two—my idea, originally—we continue giving art away for free, slowly chipping away at their sales, but like Heloise, we'll barely make a dent."

"What's option three?" None of this seems fast enough.

"We nuke 'em." Gates tosses Cicero's pages back in her direction. "We get guns, grenades, flaming arrows, and we just blow them off the planet. We have no choice. Or, we give up."

Atlas grumbles approvingly. No one else has anything to say. For a while, the only sound in the room is the low mumble of a newscaster on the media screen. The report is intercut with footage of another riot somewhere in the city. The newscaster moves her lips. People fight. The newscaster talks. People react. That's it. That's what we need to happen.

"We could expose the WI. We put the whole scam out in the open—on TV, on the radio. We let the people be the judges. This is still a democracy, right? If people see that the government and this corporation are cheating them, they'll have to do something."

"I'm with Gates." Cicero tucks her thick stack of research under her chair. "Nuke 'em. Everything's already been exposed. All the information we have is right there for anyone to see. None of this is secret. People just don't care enough to do anything about it."

"They assume—just like we used to—that the state has our best interests at heart. We thought the WI wanted to protect us. We didn't know what questions to ask. We didn't even think to ask questions.".

"Didn't we?" Cicero slumps in her chair—things have to be bad for her to give up on her posture. "Isn't that how we got where we are? If we asked questions, why hasn't everybody else? Are we so special?"

"No, we're not. That's the point. Once we found out the truth, we cared enough to try and change it. Don't you think everybody else deserves that chance—deserves to know that they've been used?"

"Say we expose them. We somehow get the word out to media screens everywhere. And then what?"

"We'll jump off that bridge when we come to it. Cicero, you love a challenge, right? Well, think of this as the ultimate test. Does everyone agree that our best bet is to expose the WI for what it really is?"

Everyone agrees that this is our best shot, but no one is convinced it will work. Not even me.

The plan is simple: Get the word out to as many people as possible. The execution won't be so easy. Cicero writes a summary of her research and sends it out to newspapers all over the nation. Edie goes back to New York and recruits some people who could make a video suitable to send to television networks. Once she's found the right talent and rounded up the right equipment, she sneaks the whole crew to D.C. and into the safe house. Atlas's little piece of the world is packed to bursting.

He seems to like it that way. He's never looked so happy as when he scrambles to accommodate the wishes of the two dozen or so rebels staying in his house. He doesn't mind cooking for an army, washing his weight in bed linens, or unclogging the toilet at least once a day. He looks happy to be busy, cooking his huge breakfasts and putting out the accompanying grease fires.

The next week is taken up recording songs and voiceovers. Atlas has dipped into some secret—even secret from Brax—bank accounts ("never trust anyone—not even family," he said during one of his darker moods). He's using the money to buy radio and television spots, while we busy ourselves recording commercials. I keep waiting for the moment when they'll ask me to be the "face" of the rebellion, but that never happens. The filmmaker, Hays, a wire-thin man with wire-rimmed glasses, declares, "The rebellion doesn't need a mascot. We'll show people the truth. The way things used to be." He finds archival footage of pre-WI concerts and fashion shows. He even finds a video of 40,000 people kissing simultaneously on the streets of Mexico City (the PDA ban is also on the rebels' list of grievances).

Voice gone hoarse, stomach rumbling with hunger, there's finally a chance to escape the makeshift recording studio (Brax's old bedroom with pillows nailed to the walls). Downstairs, I can take advantage of Atlas's lunch menu—sandwiches—and the small crowd of people eating and talking at the kitchen table. It'll be nice to hear someone else's voice for a little while.

"Any response yet?" Gates says.

"It's only been a week," Cicero says. "The papers need time to do their research. I respect that. Once the stories get printed, then we start calling for protest."

The house's spare bedroom has become a fashion design studio, and the resident designer, a girl not much older than Mouse, with spiky black hair, rushes in and out of the room taking measurements and ordering people up from their lunches to try on clothes. The protest will consist of people wearing flashy, brightly colored clothes, holding up signs and performing in front of WI headquarters here in D.C., and in front of state buildings nationwide. That is, if everything goes as planned.

"I wish we could get a hold of Heloise," Cicero says. "We could really use her help getting the word out."

"Fat chance," Gates says. "Helping us would hurt her profit margin."

"How's the boycott?" Newton says, back from a fitting.

"Not sure," Cicero says. "That's Edie's territory."

The thought of Edie, long white hair and not even owning an item of gray clothing, standing in front of a store, trying to convince civs not to go in, to trust her judgment . . . I'd laugh if my throat weren't raw from singing.

"Have you picked a day for the big protest?"

"May first. A week from today."

"And what are we supposed to do in the meantime?" Newton says.

"Find Phase II."

The chatter around the kitchen table dies down. Everyone's eyes are on me.

"Why on earth would you want to find Phase II?" Gates says.

"I think my father's there, and I know you guys will probably say no . . . but I'd really like some help finding him."

"Wait here." Cicero runs over to her stack of reports and pulls out a thick folder labeled PHASE II. "It's everything I could find."

The folder contains a printout of Cicero's research and page after page of web searches, paragraphs from ebooks, and sheets nabbed from WI files. "How long have you been working on this?"

"Ever since you told me you wanted to find your father. It's not much, but the info I found leads me to believe that Heloise was telling the truth. Phase II is right here in D.C. We shouldn't have too much trouble finding it. Getting inside, though . . ."

There's a picture of my father, from his WI file, dated only days before he disappeared. He looks like me, but with a stern face. Could he have possibly suspected what would happen?

"It'll be dangerous."

"That's why we arranged one last trip to New York." Newton grins. "Have you ever played football?"

Despite Heloise's radio silence, her son, Kepler, proves quite talkative. And once our ever-growing band of rebels manages to sneak back to New York without capture, Kepler also proves helpful at getting us a meet-up with Freud, an offensive tackle, at his compound upstate. The drive up gives us a chance to further discuss strategy and how we actually plan to discover the location of Phase II. When our creativity is exhausted ("we look for elevators with missing floors?"), Kepler takes the opportunity to give us a little more background on the man we're about to meet.

"Just Freud?" Cicero, despite her indifference to football, manages to conjure up a decent amount of interest in our host. "No last name?"

"SFL players are only given first names—easier for fans to remember and yell angrily." Newton can't wait to hang out with one of his football heroes.

"I've known him since we were little. My mom pulled some strings and the state let me go to school with the football kids." Kepler smiles. "I'm no athlete, but Freud . . .

He used to steal sports equipment and turn it into weapons. He used a lacrosse stick as a slingshot to knock birds out of the sky and he'd catch bass at night in the Potomac using a volleyball net. Then he'd set the net back up, and everyone would come in the next day wondering why the gym smelled like fish."

"What did he do with the animals?" It's hard to imagine a flock of birds following a stocky teenage football player around D.C.

"He tossed the fish back and nursed the birds back to health in his dorm room if they needed it. Back then. Now, he hides in his compound up here during the offseason and builds weapons—real weapons—bows and arrows and stuff. He still hunts. He cooks and eats what he kills."

Cicero's nose wrinkles at the thought. "I know where food comes from and everything, but actually catching and killing an animal myself . . ."

"He lives on his own terms up here." Kepler turns the car onto the road leading to Freud's house. "Completely off the grid. Makes his own clothes. Grows his own vegetables. His house is totally solar. And he wants as little as possible to do with the state, which is why he agreed to help us."

Soon, we see what Kepler means when he calls the place a "compound." To get to Freud's property, the caravan (it takes three vehicles to drive all the rebels who want training) has to turn off the interstate, onto a rocky dirt road that leads into thick woods, onto an even rockier dirt road into even thicker woods, past a hand painted sign that reads, "Private Property Keep Out Trespassers Will Be Shot", over a concrete bridge and up to a very tall gate rimmed with barbed wire at the top. Kepler rolls down his window and presses a button on a call box situated off to the side of the road.

"Private property." A voice crackles through the box.

"A wet moose walks backwards at night." Kepler manages to keep a straight face while he gives the secret code.

"But an old buzzard whistles in its sleep," comes the reply from the box, followed by a long buzz. The gate slowly slides open.

The caravan drives onto the property, the gate closing behind us as soon as the last vehicle passes through. From there, it takes only a few minutes more before we spot the series of wooden cabins that serve as Freud's house. Varying in size and shape (some are large log structures; others not much more than small huts), the cabins link to each other and the surrounding wilderness via a series of interconnected walkways, decks, and staircases.

"It's like something out of a movie." Cicero sums up what I've been thinking.

Freud steps onto the deck in front of one of the smaller huts, a trio of dead birds slung over his muscular shoulder, blood dripping down his shirt, and a grin across his broad, tanned face. He waves.

"Yeah," says Newton. "A horror movie."

Freud and Kepler exchange a handshake and a greeting before Freud addresses the group. "Welcome to my home. While you're here, consider it your home, too."

He leads us in a jog around the compound. He's only a couple years older—maybe eighteen or nineteen—but he's in much better shape. Obviously. It's his job to work out. Freud found out about the underground from a girlfriend, a cheerleader who wanted to dance without rules, and he joined the rebellion immediately.

"You get sick of losing to whoever kissed the most puppies that week. Is there anyone out there who doesn't know football's rigged?"

"When Newton first heard," Cicero whispers, "he cried."

"I want to play a fair game. If we lose because we didn't play well . . . fine. I'd just like the chance. But you're not here to hear about me, are you?"

Over the next eight hours, Freud takes us through an intensive combat training session covering everything from proper falling (never on your head) to proper blocking (never with your head). The athlete has, for some years, been learning martial arts (non-approved), and by the end of the day, he's taken a group of wimpy artists and has taught us not only how to throw a punch (thumb on the outside of the fist), but also has given us the confidence not to run should a fight come our way.

"At the end of the day, all of this will do you no good if you're up against something other than fists."

After a short walk into the woods, we come to what initially looks like a clearing. Freud flips a switch hidden in a tree branch, and suddenly floodlights shine down from beneath the canopy.

"Has anyone here ever seen a weapon before?"

Newton, Gates, and Edie raise their hands. Most of the other rebels shake their heads, no.

"Well, that's a start. What weapons have you seen and where did you see them?"

Newton goes first. "Police batons and guns. At the black market."

"You didn't buy a gun did you? Black market gun dealers never sell the real thing. Starter guns. Flare guns. Don't pull one of those out and try to take care of business unless you plan to wake up dead."

"Gun. Hers." Gates points to Edie.

Edie stands up and reaches into her jacket. She pulls out a small, pearl-handled pistol.

"Okay," Freud says. "Now there's a real piece. Where'd you get it?"

"Granny gave it to me," Edie says.

Freud laughs. "Granny! Did your grandmother teach you how to shoot it, too?"

The football player equips us all with guns, and teaches us the basics of how to use them. Then, he sets up target practice. Edie volunteers to go first, and using Granny's gun, she hits every target dead center.

"She's not my grandmother." Edie hits a person-shaped paper target in the center of its paper chest. "But she did teach me to shoot."

"Good looking—I mean good *shooting*. Who's next?"

The rest of the group doesn't perform quite as well. My shots miss everything so completely that Freud wonders if I don't need glasses. By morning, though, each person in the group has managed to hit at least one target.

Around sunrise, Freud shuts off the floodlights and leads us back inside. "I set up cots in the common room. Get some sleep. I'll be down in the bunker."

Sleep doesn't come easy these days, so why bother to claim a cot when the night's bound to be full of wandering anyway? With luck, an armchair in a hall somewhere might prove an adequate enough bed to get an hour or two of rest. First stop on tonight's wandering: the bunker. Thankfully, it's not down in a basement. Instead, Freud's bunker is a metal room on wheels connected to the back of the cabin. The heavy door hangs open, but it's probably best to knock anyway. He doesn't seem the type you want to sneak up on.

Inside the cramped metal room, the football star is half-asleep, slumped over a control panel. In front of him, a wall of media screens that show camera feeds from about twenty different cameras, including one trained on the gate where we entered the property and one showing the room we're in right now.

"I'm sorry. I didn't mean to wake you. I'll go."

"No, no." Freud sits up and wipes his face. "You're here now. Sit."

The media screens cycle through different views—the camera count is far more than twenty. No one could get anywhere near this place without Freud knowing.

"You live up here by yourself?"

"Yep. Not by choice, though."

"Really?"

"What? You thought I was a weird isolationist or something?"

"That's kind of how it looks."

"I guess you're right. This place is off-putting. I don't mean it to be."

"What about that sign out front? Trespassers will be shot."

"Yeah, trespassers, but not . . ."

"You've never brought a girl up here, have you?"

"Look, I'm a football player, right? During the season, I meet lots of girls, but I don't think I could ever bring one here."

"Wait. You've never even tried bringing a girl here? I imagined they all ran away in terror, but you've never tried? What are you afraid of?"

"I guess I didn't think there was anybody else out there who'd be interested in living the way I do."

"I think I might know someone."

"Oh yeah? Who?"

Judging by the goofy smile on his face, Freud thinks we're flirting. As attractive as he is (and he definitely is), the thought of living so far from, well, *everything* isn't exactly my idea of paradise.

"Edie. I saw the way you looked at her on the shooting range."

Freud's expression turns thoughtful. "She does know how to handle a weapon."

"I think I saw her walking around in the kitchen. She has trouble sleeping, too. Go talk to her."

Freud straightens out his wrinkled clothes as best he can and heads for the kitchen.

The wall of media screens is hypnotic as it cycles through the cameras placed all over Freud's property. So many cameras trained on something no one's supposed to ever see . . . Of course. It's so obvious.

Back in the cabin's common room, Freud and Edie are talking quietly in the kitchen. Maybe it's best not to interrupt. No, this is important.

"Hey." There's no point in talking quietly now. Everyone'll want to hear this. "I think I know where to look for Phase II."

"What?" Edie says. "How? Where?"

"What's the place in D.C. that has the most surveillance cameras?"

"The Business District." Cicero sits up on her cot and yawns. "The surveillance cameras cut down on theft, remember?"

"Where would you hide something in the city if you wanted to make sure that it was well protected and hidden, but you still wanted to keep an eye on it without being too obvious?"

"The Business District?"

"Right! If you put up your own security system somewhere out of the ordinary, people will notice, but if you use the city's own surveillance cameras . . ."

"I don't know," Cicero says. "We can't exactly go knocking on every business's door saying, 'Hi, excuse me, but do you have a secret research facility out back?' based on a hunch. We need proof. Not that your hunches aren't great, but we need a real solid lead."

"Where do we find proof?"

"We could look into the WI's financial records and see if it's spending any large sums of money on rent or electricity on a space in the Business District. But that would be the easiest thing to hide. I need to do some research. Where's your compy?"

"No interweb here," Freud says. "It's too easy for the state to track."

"Then let's go." We've learned all we can here anyway.

"Wait a minute," says Edie. "I know you're psyched to find this place, but we're all exhausted. We've been up for over twenty-four hours straight. We'll be useless if we don't get any rest. That includes you. And me."

"Stay as long as you need," Freud says. "You're safe here."

Settling into a cot to try and get some rest doesn't seem as pointless as it did a few minutes earlier. Now there's something real to do—a clue to follow up on. We're not grasping at shadows anymore.

Freud and Edie lower their voices as they continue talking for a while longer.

"I'm not surprised football is rigged," Edie whispers. "I always root for the bad guys."

Phase II must've been in the Business District this whole time, hidden in public, camouflaged by the neon lights and crowds of civs. They probably saw me on camera dozens of times, buying socks, walking in and out of Atlas Realty. When Freud and Edie's quiet conversation finally lulls me to sleep, it's restless, filled with visions of my face playing across media screens, watched by the enemy.

We stay at Freud's compound another night, getting in some extra rest (and extra target practice) before heading back to D.C. When Freud says he'd like to join the expedition and offers to arm us with as many guns as we want, responses range from Newton's "as many as I can carry" to Cicero's "I'll use my wits to keep me safe, thanks," and everything in between.

The drive back from New York is quiet—until we reach the outskirts of D.C. There's a roadblock up ahead.

"They're looking for us. They know where we've been."

"Not likely," Freud says. "They're fishing. Let's exit here."

The caravan leaves the interstate while the police lights are just blue flashes in the distance. We drive back roads until we reach the suburbs, and when we get there, we park our many cars in a shopping mall parking lot and walk the distance to Atlas's house, avoiding cameras along the way.

As soon as we set foot in the safe house, Cicero grabs her compy and runs off, probably to continue her research and find out what she can about Phase II's location. Meanwhile, the many rebels who've been living here bombard the rest of the group with questions.

"Where'd you go?"

"Where'd you get the guns?"

"Are we planning an attack?"

"You don't think they'll start shooting at protesters, do you?"

"Did you bring guns for the rest of us?"

"The guns are for a rescue mission." Edie's voice cuts through the noise. "And the details are on a need-to-know basis."

A news report pops up on the muted media screen. A senator, Jackson Lawson, III (NY) stands behind a podium, talking to the press, and Heloise stands behind him, smiling.

"Turn it up." This is probably important.

"And so, because it's wrong to tell people what they can or cannot wear on their own bodies, what they can or cannot listen to with their own ears or view with their own eyes, I am introducing a bill that will, if it passes, disband the Wagner Initiative." The senator smiles triumphantly.

"Heloise did it." Newton smiles right along with him.

The senator continues: "I have the support of several other senators, but I'm making a plea to the people of this great nation. Get your voices heard. Call your local congressperson and tell him or her that you ought to be allowed to wear your favorite color whether it is red, white, or blue! Take to the streets and show your senators that it isn't wrong to be who you are!"

"She really did do it."

My shoulders relax. (Didn't even notice they were tense.) Finally. The group of rebels around the media screen cheers.

"She hasn't done it yet." Atlas joins the small crowd, frowning. "You heard what he said. The bill has to pass the vote, and they still don't have the support they need. She likely hasn't raised enough money yet."

"What does this mean?"

It means we've all but won.

Cicero rushes over, compy in hand. "I've found it. I think I've found Phase II."

19

The safe house's back yard is quiet. With the house swarming with rebels (mostly teenagers), the noise level can roughly double that of a D.C. football game. So, in order for those of us who like a little quiet once in a while to keep our sanity, the back yard, with its overgrown garden and shady gazebo, has been designated as a noise-free zone, where you can write a song in peace, sketch quietly, or juggle without interruption.

Edie, Newton, Gates, Cicero, and I sit in the gazebo, Cicero's compy and Phase II folder on the table, along with a hastily drawn but well-detailed map of the Business District. The map indicates likely camera locations, sewer entrances, and the supposed location of Phase II (beneath what's now a taco restaurant), marked with a big red X.

"Remember when it was a gyro stand?" Cicero says.

"Yeah, and before that, it was a Chinese restaurant that never seemed to be open."

"And before that, they sold burgers," Newton says. "And they were never open."

"Right," Cicero says. "The place keeps changing from one always-closed restaurant to another, but the owner never changes."

"Let me guess," says Edie. "The WI owns the building."

"I looked up the owners of every building, hoping something like that would turn up, but the WI covered their tracks well. The building is owned by one Richard Smith."

"Helpful," Gates says. "The most common name in the country. How do you know this is the building?"

"I followed the money. Even if the Richard Smith that owns this building is a real person, which I doubt, it would be impossible to figure out which Richard Smith we're looking for. So instead, I looked up the tax records for each property within the area. I wanted to find out who pays the bills. Usually, the person or company paying the taxes is the person who owns the building. But in a handful of cases, the owner of the building and the taxpayer don't match. For all but one building, the taxpayer is a representative of the building's owner. Not the case for Richard Smith's restaurant. This little taco stand has its taxes paid by a company called Rightscope, Inc."

"Rightscope," Edie says. "Why does that sound familiar?"

"Rightscope Records. The record label that releases all of the WI's music." My hunch about Phase II being hidden in plain sight was right. Darwin's Rule #10—Trust Your Instincts. "They never expected anyone to start digging."

"So, we've found it. How do we get in?" Edie types notes on a tablet.

"That's where you and Gates come in," Cicero says. "Edie, you're familiar with New York's underground. How long do you think it would take you to become an expert on what's underneath these twelve blocks in D.C.?"

"Give me a day." Edie heads into the safe house.

"And Gates, can you find out what kind of security system they're using over there?"

"Hmmm, I'd need to go over and scout the place. Examine the cameras close up. It's risky."

"I think I know someone who can help." Kepler's going to prove even more useful than he already has. Newton hurries inside and comes back out with the photographer in tow.

"Gates. Meet Kepler. Kepler likes to take pictures. In fact, not only does Kepler like to take pictures, he likes to photograph the state with its pants down—police mess-ups, sanitation failures . . . Did you ever take any pictures of the Business District?"

"Yeah, actually. Whenever my mom would drag me down here for some SFL stuff, I'd walk around the Business District and the Pleasure District taking pictures all day. Probably got hundreds of images."

"And hidden somewhere in those images has to be at least one picture of a security camera. I'll take a look and see what I can figure out from the images." Gates and Kepler head back toward the house.

"So what should the three of us do?" Newton says.

"Not much we can do, at the moment. We need Gates' and Edie's reports before we can really come up with a plan." Nothing to do but wait. "So, let's enjoy the rest before our big finale."

It's actually too quiet outside. With the delicate spring blooms and the small groups of people lounging silently about, it feels like a still life painting. But this moment calls for movement.

"Hey! Hey everybody! Come out in the yard!"

No one seems to mind the quiet rule violation, especially when it becomes clear the plan is for National Selection to play. Setting up to go acoustic doesn't take long, and soon Newton's strumming a mandolin while Homer beats a set of bongos. I sit cross-legged singing, while dancers dance, writers write, painters paint and couples kiss in the setting sun. Atlas watches from a corner of the yard, laughing, not noticing the sky turning dark as clouds roll in.

The plan involves us doing something really, really stupid. Getting into Phase II was always going to be difficult, but the plan (concocted late one night after a heist-movie marathon, AKA "research") seems destined to fail. We'll make our big play to get into Phase II on the same day as the protest. Cicero got word to Heloise who agreed to have Senator Lawson plug the nationwide day of protest on television, so the streets will hopefully be filled with at least a few people who can serve as human camouflage.

"We'll blend in with the crowd and make our way into the Business District." Edie points out directions on the map. "When we get close enough, we'll go down into the metro station here. From there, we'll need to get through a maintenance access door, which shouldn't be too hard. We'll pick the lock. Once we're in, we'll follow the service tunnel until it ends here. See this big empty block? This is Phase II. Now see how they've cut off the other service tunnels much farther away? This tunnel butts right up against it. This has got to be an entrance."

"Which means there'll be some kind of security there," Gates says. "The main entrance is probably here, inside the taco shop, guarded heavily. But our entrance will also be protected, most likely with some kind of heavy door—probably keycard- or access code-activated. Judging by the pictures of the security cameras, they're not using state-level security. It's high-level consumer grade. We should be able to get through the door with these." He holds up several keycards. "Our magical keys to the city. They'll get us through any locked door in the building. Any door that uses a keycard, anyway." He hands out keycards and wireless headsets. "We'll communicate with these. They contain a media drive and will record video of everything that happens."

"Once we're inside, we split up into groups of two to explore and look for my father. Any guards we encounter, we'll subdue with stun guns." Everybody takes a copy of the only photo of my father I've ever seen—the one from his WI file. "Whoever finds him, leave immediately and then contact the others."

"We'll rendezvous here." Edie points to a spot on the map a few blocks away from Phase II. "It's much farther away than where we went in and closer to the safe house. A driver will pick us up."

"Then your father will tell his story to the media, and the state will have to take action." Cicero smiles.

Gates' furrows his brow. "And if—I'm sorry, Darwin, but . . . if we don't find your father?"

There it is again—that knot in my gut. He's there—he has to be there.

"Then we leave, once we're sure we've searched the place. The driver will leave exactly fifteen minutes after the first person or pair of people arrives at the vehicle." Edie's turned out to be quite a criminal mastermind. "After that, unless we hear from you, we'll assume anyone who didn't rendezvous has been captured."

Cicero outlines her strategy for spreading the word. "And then, we'll bombard the media outlets with reports that some of us have been kidnapped. We'll continue to call for protests and boycotts until the WI is ruined."

"We could be locked away for years." None of us, least of all Newton it seems, has forgotten about Franklin, sitting in prison while our plan takes shape.

"You're right." Who can blame the others for being afraid? That knot in my stomach doesn't feel like courage. "Anyone who doesn't want to do this doesn't have to. You all realize this is the moment that makes or breaks us, don't you? If we fail here . . ."

"We won't fail." Freud sat by listening for the whole meeting, but now he rallies the group like a coach in a locker room. "If any of us were failures, we'd be out there, wearing our gray clothes and listening to our toothpaste jingles happy as can be."

"Well said." Cicero puts on her best politician voice. "People like us are the ones who started painting on cave walls. We can't sit around while all of that gets erased."

20.

The sun is shining and the air is warm. You couldn't ask for a more perfect day to break into an evil corporation's secret prison. Dressed from head (green wigs are popular) to toe (sequined shoes, though impractical, stand out in a crowd) in the most colorful, regulation-violating apparel the designer was able to make, playing cheap kazoos, dancing, and singing, the thirty or so rebels headed downtown look like a hybrid circus and parade, and wouldn't have it any other way. They ride the metro into the city, careful to form a protective throng around the members of National Selection, who are, according to rumor at least, currently at the top of the state's Most Wanted list. The closer to the city center we get, the more rebels join us on the train. Soon, no one in gray can be seen within a car or two.

The rescue crew (Edie, Gates, Freud, Cicero, Newton, Kepler, Homer, and myself) gets off at the stop closest to the perimeter of the Business District. I head for the stairs to the surface.

"We don't need to go up. We can access the maintenance tunnel from down here." Edie starts for the tunnel.

The rest of the crew ignores her and instead follows close behind me up the stairs. A common, unstated urge to see the protest. Before we even reach the surface, the noise is overwhelming—chanting, singing, laughing. But that first step onto the street . . . it's better than anything any of us could have imagined.

Hundreds of people have converged on the Business District. The police have given up on keeping the crowds out of the streets, and traffic is at a standstill. People dressed in a rainbow of colors hold up signs and shout, sing, and dance. This morning, no one was sure if more than a handful of rebels would show up.

"It's like a party. Wait. Who's that?" Newton points to a stage that's been set up right in front of the taco store. A man wearing a blue suit walks toward the microphone. "Is that Senator Lawson? What's he doing here? Shouldn't he be somewhere spending Heloise's money?"

It's extremely cynical to think that all it takes to change laws in this country is money. But, here's Senator Lawson, no doubt about to give a pep talk on the rebels' behalf.

"Ladies and gentlemen. Thank you so much for joining me here." Lawson smiles and spreads his arms to the crowd. "I'm so proud to be able to share with you the freedom to dress how we want, make music if we want, kiss in public if we want." The crowd cheers. "But I want to remind you that the journey isn't over yet. We have a long road ahead of us. You need to make sure you get on the phones and let your congresspeople and your senators know how you want them to vote on what I'm calling the Free Will Act. We've got—"

"National Selection!"

"We want to hear National Selection!"

"National Selection! National Selection!"

Lawson looks around, confused. He turns to his aides on stage. "They're saying National Selection. What is that?" The microphone picks up every word.

"He doesn't even know who National Selection is!" The crowd boos even as Lawson tries to recover and continue his speech.

We've seen enough. The protest is in full swing, with or without National Selection or anyone to lead the way. The rescue team heads back down into the metro station and we head straight for the access tunnel. Edie pulls out her lockpicking tools, but the door opens without any resistance.

"Too easy."

We head into the maintenance tunnel and around corner after corner until we reach what, according to the subway plans, must be the last corner before the entrance to Phase II.

If our research has been right, then answers to all the questions I've been asking are just around the corner. There's a catch in my throat, but now's not the time for tears. Now's the time to fight.

"Hmm, bound to be a camera." Gates pulls a tablet out of the pack he's been wearing. "I'll hack into the system and record one minute of surveillance video from every camera on their grid. Then, I'll set it to play over and over in a loop on their security monitors. The cameras will still be on, but the monitors will show whatever happens for the next sixty seconds over and over again. We'll be invisible." Gates works his magic. "Let's go."

We round the corner and come face to face with the heavy entrance door. "See the camera?" Gates points to the black dome in the ceiling above the door. "Now look at my compy." The view that should have shown the eight of us huddled around Gates in front of the door instead shows an empty hallway. "And now for my next trick," Gates swipes one of his hacked keycards in the panel next to the door. With a click, the door swings open.

We've gone over this part of the mission in detail. In addition to the guns, Freud equipped us with tasers that will disable, not kill—these are our go-to weapons. The guns are emergency backups.

We go through the door, and half of us immediately start to gag. The whole place has been doused in the WI's favorite rosemary-scented bleach. We've entered at the end of a long gray hallway that branches out in several places, flanked on each side by doors with tiny windows at the top.

Cicero stands on her toes and looks through one window into the nearest cell. "It's a person."

"Check them all."

Cell after cell. Tiny window after tiny window. No sign of my father. Each room holds a bed, a table and chair, a sink and toilet, and a single prisoner dressed in gray hospital scrubs. The doors are all locked, with no place to swipe a keycard.

"Must be connected to a central system that controls the locks." Gates types away on his compy. "I'll see if I can patch into that."

The group reaches the first intersecting hallway. Cicero and Newton go left, Freud and Edie to the right. At the next intersection, Gates and Kepler go left, while Homer and I go right.

"More cells . . ." More prisoners, but still not the one we're looking for. "What is this place?"

Homer overturns a stray mop bucket and uses it as a footstool to get a better look into a cell. "These people look sick."

"Same here." Edie's words crackle through our earpieces. "They look really sick here."

"Guys, I've found something." Cicero takes over the conversation. "I'm in a lab, I think. And there's a . . . corpse that they've . . . cut open. I found some files. Patient 2330-29 . . . Status, deceased. Apparent cause of death . . . starvation. Prior to death, patient suffered from same symptoms as patients one through twenty-eight. Here's another file. Patient 2330-55. Status, alive. Patient seems to be reacting well to regimen. No signs of disorientation. No signs of violence."

"They're experimenting on people." The knot returns to my stomach. What have they done with my father?

"There's more." Cicero reads on. "Update . . . Patient now shows signs of decreased mental acuity despite daily nutrition requirements being met. Patient lashed out at research technician, biting technician's hand. It may be time to consider changing the nutritional makeup of Product Alpha."

Homer and I come to a section of Phase II that has glass walls, much like the Pleasure District's prison. Inside the first glass cell, a woman sits in a chair, staring at the wall, stroking her thinning hair. When she spots me, she calls out, and though the thick glass silences her voice, the words look like, "help me." Inside the second cell, a man, totally hairless, incredibly thin and pale, paces back and forth. The man lunges at the glass wall separating us, baring his teeth, beating on the glass. No need to panic. The glass will hold—if there's one thing the state knows how to build, it's a secure prison.

The hallway ends at another door—this one secured with a keycard lock. The keycard Gates gave me opens the door into a large, cold storeroom. Boxes labeled Product Alpha v.1.4, v.2.2, and so on line the shelves. Opening one box exposes several smaller white boxes labeled "Product Alpha Chicken Dinner." Homer opens another box, one containing syringes labeled "Product Alpha Meal Replacement Injection." This is a walk-in freezer.

"Product Alpha is food." What is the WI doing down here? "It's this stuff that's making people sick."

"Killing people more like it." Freud's voice crackles over the communication channel, saying what everyone else probably thinking.

Homer tries to open the door—no use. "We walked into a freezer and the door closed behind us. We're trapped."

The cold finally hits. My teeth start to chatter.

"I saw you go in," Edie says. "I'm close by." A rattling at the door. "My keycard's not working."

"Mine either." Freud pounds on the door.

"Sounds like they know we're inside and have reset the keycard locks," Gates says. "Everyone head for the exit. I've almost taken control of the doors."

A minute or two passes. My fingers go numb.

"Okay, everyone else here? I'm opening all the doors in three, two, one."

The door to the freezer clicks. Out in the hallway, the lights have been switched to emergency mode, flashing red. Not sure which is more frightening—the flashing red or the lingering cold numbness in my fingertips.

"Looks like they thought we'd head for the taco stand exit. Darwin, Homer, that buys you some time. Hurry. Get out of there."

174

We head back down the hallway. The doors to the rooms on either side are all flung wide open, dozens of thin, disoriented patients making their way into the hallway.

"Run."

A sick patient lunges at me but misses. Homer follows my lead toward the exit door. A few patients follow behind—the ones who weren't bedridden—jogging as best they can. They're not the only ones. Three guards have caught on and are catching up quickly.

Homer stops and turns around. "I can take them." He aims his taser at the security guards and fires, knocking one guard to the floor. He takes aim at a second guard.

"Come on!"

It's no use trying to pull him toward the exit. A gunshot sounds. Homer falls to the floor.

"Go," Homer says, trying to raise his taser with one arm, the other hanging lifeless.

"Don't be stupid."

"I'm not. You have to get out. This whole thing is about you. It's always been about you—for me, anyway."

"Homer—"

"Go," he says. "You'd do the same for any of us."

I bend down and kiss him, and then run for the door.

Homer fires his taser at one of the guards, catching him in the leg. The third guard returns fire as I push through the exit door.

Of course I'd do the same for any of them, for all of them, if it came to that. It's not stupid if it means you're doing the right thing. After all the failed plans and false leads, there's finally the some satisfaction, some relief in the knowledge that there's proof the WI is evil, and that the people in charge are about to go down, about to be locked away inside Federal Prison, where the real criminals go, where the walls aren't made of glass but of solid concrete, gray and opaque, to hide the horrors that go on inside.

"Shut the door. I can lock it behind you." Gates' voice snaps me back to the present.

"You can't lock it. Sick people are behind me. We can't leave them in there."

"Fine. Meet us at the truck."

A sprint through the access tunnel, feet pounding, breaths coming short and fast. Finally, the door to metro station is within reach. My hand reaches for the knob, fingers touch the metal, arms push the door just a little, and then—a sharp bite in my back, and I'm on floor, unable to move. Footsteps come my way, and there's the final security guard standing above me. Everything goes black.

21.

It's like a horror movie. Worse than that. It's real. To describe the feeling of waking up strapped into a wheelchair being pushed by a security guard down the winding hallways of a lab bathed in the red glow of emergency lights, still populated by sick patients, prisoners, wandering the halls in search of food, looking at you like you might be food . . . To describe it the fear, to sum it up in one tidy word—not even Cicero could do that.

What's clear is that I'm about to meet the villain, the Big Bad. If months of watching movies have taught me anything, it's that he'll be seated behind an oversized desk, wearing a monocle, smoking a cigar, and he'll explain his plan to take over the world. He'll tell me exactly how he killed my father, and threaten that if I don't cooperate, the same will happen to me. But as clearly as the scene plays out in my mind, the reality of the situation is even clearer. We can't be in Phase II anymore—we've been traveling for too long. We have to be underneath some other building in the Business District. As I'm wheeled into an elevator, the effects of the taser start to wear off. My big toe wiggles a little. My fists clench and unclench. Maybe, by force of will, my hands can slide free from the straps . . .

"If you try to escape," the guard says, "I'll have to shock you again."

"Where are we going?"

"To see the boss."

The elevator doors open, and the guard wheels me into a room that's both familiar and strange—the penthouse of Atlas Realty. The room's been cleared of its old cushy sofas, and those have been replaced with the hard, cold concrete furniture that fills the rest of the building. The stacks of newspaper have been pushed up against the walls. And there, pacing back and forth in front of the media screens, like his father used to do, is Brax.

"About time. Get her out of those straps. I don't think she's leaving. Are you?"

"So, it's true. You were on their side the whole time. Why am I here?"

"You've broken into a private research facility, and now I'm trying to decide whether to press charges."

"*You're* trying to decide? Atlas Realty owns Phase II?"

"Half of it, anyway. The other half belongs to the WI."

"But your father—"

"He didn't tell you?" A smug smile distorts Brax's face. (How did I ever find that face attractive?) "It wouldn't have made a difference anyway. He doesn't know the location of Phase II. The board of directors doesn't trust him. He disapproved of the investment from the beginning, and he's been trying to shut down the lab."

"Well, you're performing terrible experiments on people."

"I think your imagination's gotten the better of you. You've been watching too many of those horror movies. There's nothing scary about Phase II. It's market research."

"Have you been down there? Sick people. Dead bodies. Your guards killed Homer." The words catch in my throat, but now's not the time to cry—not here. I take off my headset, separate the small media drive from the rest of the device, and hand it to Brax. "See for yourself."

Brax puts the media drive in his compy, and soon audio starts to flow. He sets the media screens on the wall to play out the action. We watch together as I first discover the prisoners, then learn about the sick and hungry patients, get myself locked in the freezer, and then have to flee. We hear the sound of Homer being shot and then see my point of view as I collapse onto the tunnel floor.

Brax stops the playback. His eyes are wide and his mouth hangs open. "They said it was granola bars and milkshakes. I even toured the place, and I didn't see . . . They wanted to make us all healthy, and stop people from being overweight. Then we could move on to Phase III. They were supposed to be doing taste testing . . . with volunteers."

While Brax processes what he's just seen, a slow, calculated reach for the gun in the back of my pants proves pointless. Gone. And the taser, too. Of course the guard searched me while I was out.

"What's Phase III?"

"No one was supposed to—" Brax says. "Phase III? We're planning to change the world." Brax plops (as best he can) onto a concrete bench. "It's the next step. Once the WI has got rid of all the minor distractions—art, fatty food, football, eventually—they'll move on to Phase III: making Americans the best humans on the planet. Every citizen will be smart, physically fit, and hard-working. You'll have to pass intelligence and personality tests before you can get married or have children. All births will take place in WI hospitals."

"Is there a Phase IV?"

"In Phase IV, the government dissolves all regulations pertaining to corporations, and the WI expands business operations into Canada and Mexico—by force if necessary."

"Who's behind all this?"

"What do you mean?"

"Who's in charge? Who's the person that stands to gain from all this?"

"The person? No one. I mean, everyone. The WI's board of directors—that's like hundreds of people . . . The three million WI employees . . . And with the new grocery stores they're opening and the hospitals, that number will only grow."

"That's it?" No one's the Big Bad. Or, everyone's the Big Bad. Atlas was right all along. How can a single person be responsible for anything when the world runs on committee? "Why did you get involved?"

"Do you want the short answer or the long answer?"

"Short."

"I needed a job."

"Let's try the long answer."

"I was born into the family, the company. My father married into it. He's not really an Atlas. Unlike him, I understand what has driven my family for generations—what drives the world. And it's not nostalgia. Or art. Civilization wasn't built on beauty. It was built on money and power. Atlas Realty's board of directors knows that—that's why they overrode my father and invested in the WI. When I told the board that I was ready to take his place, they couldn't have been happier."

"Not too long ago, we were fighting all this, together, against people like you. What happened?"

My hand brushes across a lump in my back pocket. The matchbox! Somehow the guard must have missed it in his search.

"My father was always out fighting the good fight like you. He was never around to teach me how to be a man. So I had to figure it out for myself. I grew up. Maybe it's time you did, too. The WI would still take you back, you know, if I asked them to. You could be vocal director. Maybe, someday, head of the music division."

His words, the words of a boy who spends every waking hour cooped up inside his father's office, staring at media screens, playing at being a man, aren't even a little bit tempting. The Darwin who would have given anything to be the most important singer in the WI is gone, just as surely as the Brax who rode a hydrobike and partied every night and fought against the system and made me care about him no longer exists. Maybe he never really existed at all.

"As childish as it may sound, I still believe in beauty. And I also believe that when people find out about Phase II—"

"Not happening." Brax pulls the media drive out of the computer, throws it on the floor, and then crushes it with his foot.

"You can't be serious." Slowly, I work the matchbox out of my pocket. "You'd let them get away with murder? Are you really that far gone?"

"Don't be so melodramatic. All those people you saw signed release forms. They volunteered—I'm sure of it. Any side effects they experienced were purely accidental."

"Death is quite a side effect. Anyway, there are more media drives out there. Mine wasn't the only one."

"The security guard told me there was a group of you. He called for backup, and I can guarantee we've tracked the rest of you down by now. They're all probably joining your friend Homer in custody right now."

"Homer's alive?"

"Alive and headed for prison. And so are the rest of your friends. Tell me: Are you willing to go to jail and throw your life away on a silly rebellion or do you want to become part of something even bigger?"

I already am a part of something big. And going to jail isn't going to change that. Is this the choice my father had to make?

"Do you know what happened to my father?"

"He fell off a boat. Isn't that what you told me? You've got to forget about all your conspiracy theories. No villain—no bad guy hiding in the shadows." Brax presses an intercom button. "Guard, when Ms. Singer reaches the bottom floor, please take her into custody and turn her over to the police."

One last examination of Brax fails to reveal a part of him that seems willing to listen to reason. His eyes look just as sad and beautiful as the first time we met, but now there's no mystery there, no rebel hidden inside.

I strike a match, and as the flame grows, Brax's eyes get wide. He's never seen fire in person before.

"What's that? What are you doing?"

"Your father left enough newspaper in here to light up this whole room. I bet you, by the time the fire department gets here, the whole building will be lit up. No more Atlas Realty equals no more partnership with the WI. Without your money, they might even go out of business."

"You'll kill us both."

"What do you care? Like you said, it's not about you or me. It's about something bigger, right?"

"You wouldn't dare."

The picture on the matchbook has faded, but the message is still clear. No matter what Homer says, this shouldn't be just about me. It should be about the rebellion—about right and wrong. Burning down Atlas Realty, killing myself along with Brax, won't solve the problem, and it won't bring back my father.

"There may not be any bad guys, but I'm still one of the good guys."

With the match blown out, the only thing left to do is turn myself in. I've gotten the answers I was after—even if they're not the ones I hoped to hear.

22.

From inside thick glass walls, the Pleasure District's neon lights glow even brighter than normal. This is what it's like inside the D.C. jail. Watching other people have fun really is torture. Even though the building is supposed to be soundproof, laughter rises up from the streets. Or maybe the state pipes the sound in through hidden speakers. That wouldn't be surprising at all. Sleeping on the small, hard cot isn't so bad, but the food . . . After a week of eating stuff that probably tastes worse than cardboard, you start to wonder if you might prefer a Phase II meal replacement injection.

My mother comes to visit every day. On day one, she gets the full story leading up to this moment.

"Breaking and entering. That's how they got me."

On day three, Mom brings a message from Heloise via Atlas the elder: "I understand my son has gotten himself arrested along with the rest of you. I'm paying for a lawyer for him. Would you like me to cover your costs as well? The tour continues as ever, but we're not making enough money to get the votes we need in Congress. I hoped your end of things would have greater success."

On days four, five, and six, we spend the better part of the visit making small talk about the weather. Today, though, there's news.

"They've done it." Mom smiles. "They've put you on TV."

"Who has?"

"The rebels. Watch."

Mom pulls out her celly and pulls up a video. A title plays across the screen: Inside Phase II.

"This is the footage from last week. How? Brax destroyed all of the media drives."

"The man who made the video—"

"Hays?"

"That's his name. He told me everything recorded on your media drives was streaming back to the safe house and recorded on a hard drive there. The footage arrived safe and sound. All he had to do was edit it together."

"This is incredible. So Atlas paid for the airtime?"

"This is the part you'll love. They sent the video out to the TV stations. No letters, no money. And the TV stations are airing it—every single one of them. Special Investigative Report. Breaking News. They're calling for criminal charges to be filed."

An alarm sounds. Visiting hours are over.

No party, protest, or parade the rebels ever staged compares to the circus outside the courthouse the morning of my trial. The plaza out in front of the massive white building teems with rebels decked out in colors, police trying to subdue them, and reporters intent on capturing all the action.

Walking up the courthouse steps in an outfit Mom picked out (a plain gray skirt and jacket, on the advice of the lawyers—one of them anyway) is more intimidating than walking onto any stage. Heloise's lawyer, a stern-looking woman in a dark gray suit, insists the outfit will show my remorse. The lawyer Atlas hired thinks wearing all gray is a sign of weakness, and thus showed up in bright green.

My friends and I, plus our parents, several prison guards, and the two lawyers push our way through a crowd of rebels showing their support with signs and songs and reporters shouting questions and shoving microphones and cameras in our faces. The noise is so much that I only hear one question:

"Who do you think will be found guilty today? You or the WI?"

Before any answers can be given, the crowd abruptly shifts away from our group and over to another group of people arriving at the courthouse. The top-ranking members of the WI. Their faction is even larger than mine—it looks like they have a team of six or seven lawyers in addition to the familiar faces from Croon's trial. The head of the WI and other big shots.

"Their trial begins today, too." Atlas's lawyer straightens his green tie. "Hopefully, we can get yours over with quickly so I can go and watch theirs."

Sound echoes in the large, empty room where our trial is supposed to take place. It looks like a movie set—wood and fabric everywhere, beautiful and terrifying.

"Why'd they put us in such a big room?" Homer's been shot but not badly wounded. His arm hangs in a sling. What happened in the hallway—that kiss—hasn't really been talked about. Was it the right thing to do? Felt like it at the time. Will it happen again? Hard to say, but when Homer showed up this morning, I hugged him tight, trapping his injured arm between us and making him flinch in pain.

"They thought you'd have a big audience." Heloise's lawyer methodically unpacks her briefcases, laying pens and notebook on the table at right angles. "But it seems a more interesting show has been booked across the hall."

The WI officials walk past the doorway and into the courtroom opposite this one, followed by what seems like an endless stream of rebels and reporters. A single person walks into our courtroom and sits near the back—Franklin. He waves.

Newton waves back. "Franklin's free!"

"You're welcome." Atlas's lawyer doesn't see the dirty look Newton sends his way.

Soon enough, it's time to take the stand and retell the events that led to my arrest. The part about the sick patients and the experiments makes some of the jurors look like they might lose their lunch. Other parts of the story I have to tell twice—bursts of loud booing from across the hall drown me out.

My friends take the stand, one by one recounting their own versions of the same events, and with each new person, the shouts from across the hall grow louder and louder. Finally, Homer relays the story of his gunshot wound—the fear, then the sound, then the pain. By now the noise across the hall has become deafening. Both sides decline closing arguments, and the judge nearly has to yell to make herself heard as she gives the jury the order to deliberate.

The next hour is the longest hour ever. Maybe the sentence won't be so bad—the maximum for breaking and entering is only twenty years—I'd be thirty-six when I got out, still young in some parts of the world . . .

"I'm sorry." Cicero hugs me. "I'm sorry I nagged you so much." Cicero's eyes shine with tears.

"Don't get all weepy on me, now. We could win this thing."

"But just in case. I'm sorry I turned you in that time for not making your bed."

We've been barfed on, we've shot guns, and we've broken many, many laws since then, but Cicero is still thinking about some out of place sheets. Funny. It seemed so important back then.

"I deserved it. I knew you liked things neat and . . . I'm sorry I got you into this mess."

The jury comes back in and takes their seats. The noise across the hall seems to subside.

"How do you find?" The judge holds her gavel at the ready.

One of the jurors stands up. She looks familiar. A rebel? Or maybe someone who sold me a pair of socks once or twice . . .

"We find all the defendants," the juror says, "not guilty."

A cheer rivaling any noise from across the hall rises up. A weight is gone from my shoulders. When everyone in the room has hugged nearly everyone else, I feel a hand on my back. A courthouse bailiff stands behind me.

"Ma'am," he says. "I need you to come with me." He leads me toward the door.

"Not without me," both lawyers say in unison, trailing after us.

"That won't be necessary," says the bailiff, as he opens the door to the courtroom across the hall where the WI trial is taking place.

The standing-room only crowd parts in front of us, the bailiff leading me toward the front of the courtroom. There's Croon in the back, and there's Atlas sitting next to him—so that's why he skipped our trial. My friends follow me into the courtroom and squeeze into the back of he crowd while I push through to the front. Snatches of conversation pierce through the noise of the murmuring crowd.

"That's her."

The bailiff stops in the spot between the prosecution's table, with its two lawyers representing the state, and the defense's table, with fifteen or so people packed behind it, including Brax. Beads of sweat roll down the WI director's face and drip onto his expensive-looking suit. He looks even sleazier in person than he does in his portraits hanging all over WI headquarters.

A prosecutor stands up. "The state calls to the stand: Darwin Singer."

The faces of the men and women who stole my life and the lives of so many others look up to the witness stand, their eyes pleading for mercy. They want me to lie, to say it wasn't that bad, that no one's to blame really, and that things are the way they are because that's the way society runs—by committee.

"Will the witness please state her name and tell us her history with the Wagner Initiative?" the prosecutor says.

"My name is Darwin Singer, and I'm a musician—an artist."

My voice trembles. Now's the time to put into words all the horror that's happened to me. But the words are stuck in my throat. I take a moment (Never Let 'Em See You Sweat), and the whole courtroom silently waits for me to continue. A snatch of a tune floats in through the window from the courtyard below, bringing with it a reminder of all the people outside (all the people everywhere) singing at this very moment. They need someone to speak for them. It's about them—not about me.

"WI recruiters take kids from their homes when they're as young as three years old."

A WI lawyer jumps to his feet. "Objection! The witness can't testify on events she wasn't there to see."

The judge motions for the lawyer to sit down. "Ms. Singer, please just tell us what happened to you, as it relates to the WI."

"I'll do my best . . . But this isn't just my story. It's our story. Yours and mine. It's the story of anyone who's ever sung or danced or written a poem or sketched a doodle in the back of a notebook. It's the story of art and passion and greed. Honestly, if I hadn't lived it, I don't know if I'd believe it myself. Because . . . I never thought such things could exist. I always thought human nature was good and tidy. But it's not. All of us, we're messy, desperate, self-centered creatures. And that chaos and desire—that's where art comes from. That's what makes us beautiful. It also makes us ugly. So I guess this story concerns the ugly side of human evolution. The need to go on, to feed yourself, to make money, to do a job. One day, about thirteen years ago, an employee followed an order."

Nadria Tucker was born in Atmore, Alabama and grew up living the small-town Southern life, which had a great influence on her work. She received an English degree from Auburn University before getting her master's in creative writing at UAB. She is the author of *The Heaviest Corner on Earth*, a collection of short stories set in and around Birmingham, Alabama, where Nadria lives. You can find her online at nadriatucker.com.

www.darwinsinger.com

Cover art © 2012 by Jamie Harper

Sixteenth Avenue Books